As she dragged the can the rest of the way to the curb, Becky was thinking so hard that she was barely aware of how much stronger the rotting smell that had hung around all day was getting. When she reached the curb, though, it flooded her senses so much that she had to let go of the can to cough and cover her face with her hands. It was heavy and foul, even worse than it had been the night before.

Suddenly, from the sidewalk beside her came a thick, wet-sounding snarl.

A small animal was coming toward her slowly, its green eyes shining unnaturally in the glow from the streetlights. She realized that it was dragging its left hind leg behind it, moving painfully. Becky froze as the creature came closer to her, stepping into the light.

ROTTEN APPLE BOOKS

Mean Ghouls by Stacia Deutsch

Zombie Dog by Clare Hutton

Zombie Dog

by Clare Hutton

ROTTEN
APPLE

SCHOLASTIC INC.

For James, Fiona, and Matt, with whom I would
face zombies any day.

ISBN 978-0-545-39824-4

12 11 10 9 8 7 6 5 4 3 2 1   12 13 14 15 16 17/0

Printed in the U.S.A.   40
First printing, August 2012

Chapter One

"I'm coming to get you!" Becky Nolan called. Her two-year-old Labrador retriever, Bear, whuffed excitedly behind his mouthful of purple octopus toy and barreled down the porch steps.

Becky leaped down the steps after Bear and grabbed hold of two of the stuffed octopus's legs, pulling the toy toward her as her dog set his legs and growled playfully.

They yanked the octopus back and forth for a few seconds, until Bear suddenly dropped his head and whined softly.

Becky automatically let go of the stuffed toy and reached for Bear. "What's the matter, sweetie?" she asked softly, patting his glossy black side. "What's up, boy?"

Bear danced backward out of reach, the octopus clutched triumphantly in his mouth. His eyes were shining and he was grinning a big doggy grin: Becky was sure that he was laughing at her.

"That dog is *so* the boss of you," Becky's best friend, Charlotte, said from the porch. She was laughing at Becky, too. "Look at how he outwitted you."

"Naughty boy," Becky said. She lunged playfully toward him, but Bear quickly dodged away from her. A minivan pulled up in front of the house. From inside, Charlotte's mom waved to them.

"Gotta go," Charlotte said, pulling her backpack onto her shoulders and tightening her ponytail. "See you at school tomorrow."

Becky stared at the minivan with dismay. "You just got here!" she complained.

Charlotte laughed. "We did homework together and made brownies and you showed me your new clothes and we talked and played with Bear," she reminded Becky. "I've been here for ages."

"I know," Becky agreed. "I just miss hanging out with you all the time."

The year before, when Becky's family first moved to this town, her family had rented an apartment on the street where Charlotte lived. Charlotte had come over almost every afternoon. But over the summer, Becky's family had moved to this new house on Tulip Street, which her parents called their dream house, and now it felt like she hardly saw Charlotte outside of school. "Maybe you can spend the night this weekend?" Becky asked.

Charlotte's mom beeped her horn impatiently.

"Maybe," Charlotte said, moving off toward the minivan. "That house next door to you is pretty creepy looking, though. I might be too scared to sleep here." She made a joking grimace as she pulled open the passenger door.

"Wait, what?" Becky said. Charlotte waved and climbed into the minivan, slamming the door as her mother pulled out.

Becky blinked in confusion at the back of the van and then climbed slowly back up her porch stairs. She looked over at the empty house on the other side of the fence. Creepy? It was just an empty house. Her parents called it the "old McNally house," but she didn't know who the McNallys were, or had been.

Becky sat on the porch swing to think. The McNally house had clearly once been a pretty house like the others on the street. But now it was obviously neglected — its paint was peeling and the windows were boarded over.

Becky could see why Charlotte thought it was creepy. The house was pretty dilapidated, and the yard was overgrown. Thick dark evergreens grew close around the walls of the house. Altogether, it looked as if something had been shut up inside it, something that might try to get out, and the trees and boards were there to hold it back.

The chains on Becky's porch swing creaked as she swayed, and she almost thought she heard an answering *creak* from the other house.

She stilled the swing and listened. Nothing.

Another *creak* came from somewhere in the old house on the other side of the fence. The late afternoon light dimmed as a cloud passed over the sun, and, suddenly chilled, Becky shivered.

She automatically began to reach out for the comforting warmth of Bear's thick fur, but didn't find it. Where *was* Bear?

"Oh *no*," she muttered. "Dad's going to *kill* me."

Ever since the Nolan family had moved to their new house, Bear had made a habit of cheerfully trotting off to visit the neighbors whenever he could — and sometimes he came back with a souvenir. Mrs. Baxter down the street had been *so* mad when Bear stole the cushions from her lawn furniture and dragged them through a bush, and when she'd complained to Becky's parents, they'd made Becky replace them with her own money.

Becky had begged for a dog for years before they'd gotten Bear. She'd promised that she would take care of everything her dog needed. But her parents had been really reluctant, especially her dad. He thought a dog would be too much work and inconvenience for everyone.

When her parents had finally broken down and given her Bear for her eleventh birthday, he had been a soft, round, little bear cub of a puppy who had squirmed in her arms and eagerly strained to reach and lick her chin and face, giving happy puppy yips the whole time. She and Bear had been crazy about each other from first sight. But her dad still sighed and rolled his eyes whenever Bear got into trouble. And now that they lived in a house with a big yard for Bear to run around in, he expected Bear to behave better than he had in the apartment.

"Bear!" Becky called, standing up to scan the neighborhood. "Where are you, boy? Come on home!"

She was peering off toward the far end of the street when she heard Bear's license tags jingling. Turning, she saw him trotting up the driveway. He was clearly proud of himself; his ears looked perky and his tail was straight up in the air. Becky breathed a sigh of relief. At least she wasn't going to have to spend the evening looking all over the neighborhood for him. "You'd never go too far when it's almost dinnertime, huh, boy?" she said affectionately, and Bear, understanding the word *dinner*, sped up.

There was something in his mouth, though — a ball. Becky held out her hand and he dropped it into her palm, not fighting her this time, and then barked eagerly, as if expecting her to throw it for him.

Ugh. The ball was about the size of a tennis ball, and it might have been blue once, with a pattern of stars or dots, but it was filthy and ripped now. There was a patch of greenish mold growing on it, and Becky almost gagged at the nasty, rotting smell it gave off. He'd probably dug it up somewhere. "Yuck, Bear," Becky said, holding it gingerly between two fingers. "That better not make you sick."

At least no one will be mad that he took this, she thought. Holding the ball away from her body, she dropped it in one of the trash cans at the end of the driveway.

Thunder rumbled overhead, and Becky looked up in surprise. It had been such a beautiful, sunny afternoon a few minutes ago, but now the sky was filled with ominous black clouds. Another *crack* of thunder came, and Bear pressed against Becky's legs, trembling a little. He hated thunderstorms.

"It's okay, sweetie," Becky said uneasily. She usually liked thunderstorms, but it was strange how this one had sprung up from nowhere.

A flash of lightning lit up the sky. Becky grabbed hold of Bear's collar, and they ran together toward the house. Thunder cracked once more as she threw open the front door, and Bear whined.

Letting go of his collar and closing the front door, Becky breathed a sigh of relief. They'd gotten into the house before it started raining, luckily: Wet dogs stunk. "It's okay, Bear," she said comfortingly again, and petted his head. Bear whimpered loudly.

"What's the matter with Bear?" her mom called from the living room.

"He's scared of the thunderstorm," Becky called back. She pulled out an old towel from a basket near the door and wiped the dirt from the yard off Bear's feet, then took off her own shoes. Bear followed her, his tail wagging lazily and his fears apparently forgotten, into the living room.

"Thunderstorm?" her mom asked, frowning at her quizzically over the book she was reading on the couch. "What are you talking about?"

Behind her, sunshine streamed through the windows.

Becky blinked in surprise. "It was thundering a minute ago," she said. "And it looked like it was really going to pour."

"How strange," her mom said. "I didn't hear anything. Did you and Charlotte get your homework done?"

"Uh-huh," Becky said. She flopped down in a chair and stared out the window. Bear rested his head on her leg, and she petted him absently. Outside the window, the sky was bright and blue and peaceful.

Weird.

Chapter Two

The next day in social studies class, Becky stretched, yawned, and doodled a dog's head on the corner of her notebook page. She gave it quizzical eyebrows, floppy triangular ears, and a grinning mouth. Bear's friendly face looked back up at her.

With a rueful smile, Becky added a ring of ripped cushions and uprooted plants around her drawing. Even she had to admit that her Bear was such a naughty dog sometimes. But *so* cute, and so sweet and loving. Such a good dog in all the ways that mattered. Becky felt happy just thinking about Bear. She yawned again and looked around the room.

Lots of the other kids were doodling, too, or staring off into space. Even though it was mid-September and two weeks into seventh grade, it was still as warm as summer outside, and the smell of hot grass came through the classroom windows, reminding Becky of the long, lazy days of August. The voice of Mr. Clauson, their social studies teacher, was just a steady drone in the background, easy to ignore.

Becky shaded in the dog's face and turned in her seat to show it to Charlotte. But Charlotte was looking straight ahead, her brown eyes fixed attentively on the teacher, and didn't notice.

Sighing, Becky turned her own attention back to her drawing.

"Okay, everybody, take a minute and partner up," Mr. Clauson said, breaking her concentration. "Oral presentations will start on Monday, and I expect you to have some kind of visual aids." Becky stiffened. Clearly, she had missed something.

"Partner up for what?" Becky whispered frantically to Tonya Zimmerman, who was sitting in front of her.

"Mythology," Tonya whispered back. "Everybody's supposed to pick either a historical or modern myth system and do a report on it."

Becky automatically looked to her left, but Charlotte had her back turned to her and was talking to Lila Kenzie on her other side.

"Char?" Becky said.

Charlotte glanced back at Becky. "Oh, uh," she said awkwardly. Her cheeks flushed. "Lila and I were thinking we'd talk about Northwest Indian myths. She used to live in Seattle, and her parents have some books and stuff about them."

"Wait," Becky said, confused. "But I thought we'd — we always do projects together!"

Charlotte shifted in her chair and tucked a stray wisp of hair back behind her ear. "I know," she said, "but Lila and I thought it would be fun to work together on this one."

Becky's heart sank right down to the bottoms of her shoes. Why would Charlotte not want to be her partner? Was Charlotte mad at her? Last year they'd always done everything together, but this year Charlotte had already joined chorus and was talking about trying out for the drama club's musical, even though Becky couldn't carry a tune. And she hadn't been interested in joining art club, even though Becky was really excited about it.

Charlotte bit her lip and gave Becky a small guilty smile. "Next time, okay, Becky?" she said, and turned back around toward Lila. There was something weird about that smile, Becky thought. Was there something Charlotte wasn't saying?

Looking around, Becky tried to catch Tonya's eye, but the dark-haired girl had started talking to the girl next to her about whether they should do their report on Bigfoot or Greek myths.

In fact, Becky realized as she looked around the classroom, all of her friends were already partnered up with other people. Her heart started to beat faster. It was almost as if they were ignoring her on purpose, she thought.

What if everyone had decided they didn't like her anymore, and she hadn't found out about it until now?

"Okay, everybody," Mr. Clauson said from the front of the room. "I'm passing around the sign-up sheet. Each team needs to write down what they'll be doing their presentation on."

"Can we do monster myths from different cultures?" Paul Greenberg asked from the back of the room. "Like, could I look at how zombie stories are told in different societies?"

"Absolutely," Mr. Clauson said. "It can be fascinating to find similarities that show up across cultures."

He went on about different kinds of myths that turned up over and over again around the world, but Becky was barely listening. When the sheet landed on her desk, she stared at it in dismay. How had this happened? She'd thought the class was full of her friends, and now she didn't even have a partner for the report. Was she the only one left?

There was a flash of white, and a folded note landed on her desk. When Becky looked up, Nate — her new neighbor from Tulip Street — gave her a little half wave from a few seats away. Becky unfolded the note and read:

Want to be partners? We could do Egypt: cats and mummies!

Becky hesitated for a split second. Why did Nate want to be her partner? He seemed totally nice, but she really barely knew him. Then she shrugged, sighed with relief, nodded to Nate, and wrote down *Becky Nolan, Nate Wikowski, Egyptian myths.* She didn't care what they did, she just didn't want to have to do the presentation alone. At least *everybody* didn't hate her.

After class, Becky stopped at her locker to drop off her books before heading for the bus. Charlotte came up next to her and peered into the mirror inside her locker door.

Becky didn't know why Charlotte was bothering: She looked as neat and put together as she always did, from her tight blond ponytail and tiny touch of pink lip gloss (the only makeup her parents would let her wear) to her clean pink sneakers and socks folded down exactly the same amount at the top.

Glancing at the bits of her own reflection she could see behind Charlotte's, Becky sighed. Her wavy dark hair was frizzing up from the heat, freckles spattered across her cheeks, and she glimpsed a smear of purple paint across her nose that must have been there since art class that morning. In contrast to Charlotte's neat preppy outfit, Becky's green T-shirt looked sloppy and the hems of her jeans were ragged.

"Did you take notes during math class?" Charlotte asked, tightening her ponytail. "I'm not sure I understood what Mrs. Michaels was saying about angles." She had the assignment down perfectly, Becky was sure, but Charlotte always liked to double-check things.

"Yeah, I got it — you can just call me if you have trouble with the homework," Becky said. She hesitated and then asked, "Charlotte, are you mad at me or something?"

"Of course not!" Charlotte stared at her, her brown eyes wide. "Why would you think that?"

She looked sincere, but Becky still had that little wriggle of anxiety deep in her stomach. "Then how come we hardly hang out anymore?" she asked, realizing as she said it how true it was. "Yesterday was the first time you'd come over in ages. And you never ask me over to your house."

Charlotte frowned. "You know my parents don't let me have anyone over when they're working."

And your parents work all the time, Becky added silently. Out loud, she said, "But you used to come over to my old house a lot."

Charlotte looked at Becky for a moment, frowning a little as if she was trying to work something out. Then she seemed to make up her mind. "Look, Becky," she said. "I'm sorry, it's not you. I'm still your friend. I'm just — sometimes I'm hanging out with people from chorus. And you live far away now. Plus" — she hesitated, gave a little crooked smile, and continued in a half-joking voice — "your new house is creepy."

Becky shook her head. Her family's new house was *not* creepy. It had four bedrooms and a wide wraparound porch big enough to hang out on, and the flower beds in front were full of late roses and pansies. The kitchen was sunny and spacious, and there were two fireplaces, one in the living room and one in the dining room. Out back was a big fenced-in yard for Bear.

"It is *not*. It's a nice house," she said, hurt.

"Well, *your* house isn't creepy," Charlotte said, looking back into Becky's mirror and automatically straightening her collar. "But it's right next door to the McNally house. Like I said yesterday, I don't know how you can sleep at night with it just outside your window."

A guy's voice came from behind them. "The McNally house?" he asked.

Becky and Charlotte turned around to see a couple of eighth grade boys, Tyler and Will, staring at them.

"Becky lives next door to the *McNally house* now?" Tyler said, grinning.

Will started to laugh. "Are you serious?" he said. "Why would you move there?"

Other people had overheard Tyler, and Becky realized that a small circle of people was gathering near them. Becky looked around at them all. "What's going on?" she asked, confused. "What are you guys talking about?"

Charlotte grabbed hold of her wrist. "I didn't want to tell you this, Becky," she said, her brown eyes wide and apologetic, "but there are all kinds of rumors about the McNally house. Everybody thinks there's something *wrong* with it. No one's lived there for years."

"What kind of rumors?" Becky asked, feeling hot and uncomfortable. Everyone was giggling and staring at her with wide, amused eyes.

"Well," Charlotte said, and swallowed nervously, "like that it's the headquarters for a werewolf pack."

A sixth grade girl in the circle around them nodded eagerly. "I heard they transform in the basement there every full moon."

Paul from Becky's social studies class broke in. "No, a scientist used to live there who wanted to learn how to bring back the dead. Instead, he ended up making zombies and other monsters." He lowered his voice ominously. "And some people say these vicious creatures still roam the neighborhood at night."

Tonya shivered. "My little brother wouldn't even trick-or-treat on your street last year," she said.

"No," said Lila, tightening her own perfect ponytail, "I always heard that there was a headless ghost haunting the McNally house." She gave Becky a superior little smile. "*I* wouldn't want to spend the night anywhere near there."

Charlotte winced and squeezed Becky's arm reassuringly, but Becky felt like her insides were frozen. She looked slowly around the circle at everyone's faces. Some of the people around her were laughing, some were looking at her pityingly, and some were making exaggerated expressions of horror.

Apparently her parents' dream house was actually a total nightmare.

Chapter Three

"I'm sorry, but mummies are just gross," Becky said. "Can you believe they pulled people's brains out through their noses? Disgusting!"

"Well, they didn't do it while the people were alive," Nate said mildly from the other side of the porch table. He'd come over to work on their project that Friday after school. He pushed his shaggy brown hair out of his eyes and grinned at her. He really was pretty cute, Becky realized. She'd known who he was since she moved to town last year, but they'd never talked much.

"How come you asked me to be your partner for this?" she asked, and then felt her cheeks heat up. Sensing her tension, Bear sat up from where he had been lying at her feet and pushed his cool nose against her hand. She gave him a pat.

"I just thought it might be fun," Nate answered. "You seem pretty cool." He started to flush, too, and Becky noticed a spray of freckles across his cheeks. "Not to mention that your drawings are going to make our presentation the best," he added. "That mummy cartoon is hilarious."

"Thanks," Becky said, smiling. Bear thumped his tail twice against the floor of the porch, stood up and circled around, then lay down again contentedly.

A breeze rustled the branches of the evergreen trees next door, and Becky glanced toward them. It almost felt like the McNally house was looking back at her, its boarded windows like unfriendly eyes, and she tried to push the feeling away.

"Have you heard any stories about the McNally house from kids at school before?" she asked Nate.

"About how it's haunted and full of vampires and zombies?" he asked. Becky nodded. "Yeah," he said. "Nobody really believes them, though. I know I don't. I've never seen anything unusual about it."

"But doesn't it bother you when people say our street is creepy?" Becky asked.

"Nah," Nate said. "They're just kidding around." Becky nodded. She'd have to try to look at it that way.

Becky's nine-year-old brother, Jake, opened the door and wandered out onto the porch, holding an apple. "I'm bored," he said cheerfully. "What're you guys doing?"

Nate pushed the poster board that had been lying on the table between them toward him. "Isn't your sister a good artist?" he asked.

"Yeah, these are funny," Jake agreed, and took a loud, crunchy bite of his apple. "So they let you just draw mummy cartoons for homework in middle school?" Without waiting for an answer, he looked around. "Hey, where's Bear?"

Becky glanced toward the floor, where Bear had been flopped a few minutes before, and her heart dropped like a stone. The big dog was gone.

She stared at Jake and Nate, who were looking wide-eyed back at her. Jake gave a low whistle. "Mom and Dad are going to *kill* you," he said.

"Bear! *Bear!* Come on, boy!" Becky shouted, almost in tears. She, Nate, and Jake had split up to look for

Bear and she'd already checked his favorite spots: under Mrs. Baxter's forsythia bush, in the sunny spot in the middle of the little kids' playground a couple of blocks away, and outside the back door of the family at the end of the street who ate a lot of burgers. She didn't know where to look next. Jake had recruited the Kolodny kids from across the street to help look, and Becky could hear them yelling for Bear from the next block.

After circling the block, Becky came to a halt back in front of her own house. She bit her lip and gazed up and down the street, half expecting to see Bear trotting happily toward her, clutching something in his mouth that didn't belong to him. Where could he be? He had never gone so far that she couldn't find him before, or not come when she called. Becky blinked away the stinging in her eyes.

Next door, the McNally house was quiet and dark. Becky walked toward it hesitantly and laid her hand against the boards of the high fence around the house. What if Bear had gotten in there somehow? He could be trapped inside. Maybe she should check.

Becky noticed a loose board in the corner of the fence. Maybe Bear had gone through there. If Becky pushed it aside, she would be able to slip through into the yard. She hesitated, her heart beating hard.

Going into the McNally yard would be trespassing. Her parents would be really mad if they found out.

And there were all those creepy stories about the place. They were ridiculous, of course, but . . . Becky looked up at where the upper story of the house loomed above the fence. It looked dark and dank and horrible.

Still, she could picture Bear, frightened and alone in the dark. Maybe he had fallen through a basement window and couldn't get out.

"Hey," Nate said, coming down the sidewalk toward her. "He's not over by the elementary school."

Becky looked up at the McNally house again. "I'm afraid he might have gotten under the fence," she said anxiously.

Nate made a face. "You think Bear went ghost hunting?" he joked. When Becky just looked at him, he got serious quickly. "I'll come with you," he said determinedly. "I've got your back."

Becky nodded, her mind made up, and put out her hand to pull back the loose board.

"Hey! Becky!" The call came from down the street, and Becky jerked her hand away, letting the board fall back into place. Turning, she saw — hooray! — Bear, jogging down the street toward her and looking pleased with himself. Tonya was with him, holding on to his collar. Both Nate's buddy Noah and Robin, another girl from their class, were with them.

Becky ran toward Bear and dropped to her knees, wrapping her arms around her dog's neck. "Oh, thank you," she said to the other kids. "Where did you find him?" Bear wiggled in her arms and licked her face, and she laughed and tightened the hug.

"He showed up on our street," Tonya said, "and your name and address were on his tags, so we thought we'd walk him back over to you."

"Thank you *so* much," Becky said again, climbing to her feet. Just saying thank you didn't seem like enough to show how grateful she was. "Do you guys want to stay for dinner? We were going to cook out, and my mom won't mind a couple more kids."

Robin and Tonya looked at each other. "Are you sure it's okay?" Robin asked.

"Oh yeah, my mom loves having our friends over." Becky saw Tonya and Robin glance at each other again, and then over toward the McNally house. Maybe they hadn't been asking if staying for dinner was okay with Becky's mom, but had meant *okay* like *not scary.* "It's fine," Becky assured them.

"Sounds awesome," Noah said, and headed for the steps up to Becky's porch. After a moment, Tonya and Robin followed him.

"You found Bear!" Jake came running down the street toward them, trailed by the two Kolodny kids, Danielle and Peter, who were about his age.

They all petted Bear and fussed over him, and he wagged his tail eagerly, loving the attention.

As the younger kids started heading toward the house, Peter accidentally shoved into Jake, who reached out a hand and steadied himself against the fence outside the McNally house. Bear stiffened suddenly and dashed between Jake and the fence. Leaning against Jake's legs, he *shoved*, pushing Becky's little brother away from the fence.

"Bear!" Jake scolded, laughing. "Don't push!" Grabbing hold of Bear's collar, he followed the Kolodny kids toward the house.

Becky stared at their backs. Bear's tail was cheerfully wagging again, and Jake reached his other hand over to tousle the dog's ears.

It had almost been like Bear was protecting Jake, pushing him away from something dangerous. *But he must just be hungry and hurrying Jake along*, Becky thought. *There can't* really *be something wrong with the old house, can there?*

"Uno!" Noah shouted, holding his last card up. Game play went around the circle again, and he slammed the card down in triumph.

Becky laughed and started to gather the cards together. Everybody had gorged on the burgers and hot dogs her parents had grilled up, and then they'd settled on the porch to talk and play games as the sun set. Jake and the Kolodny kids were kicking a ball back and forth in the yard, Bear galumphing around after them, barking happily.

Next to Becky, Tonya turned away from the finished card game and blew bubbles at the younger kids from a bottle of bubble liquid she'd found on the porch. Danielle and Peter both jumped to smack at the bubbles floating over them, and Jake grabbed the opportunity, kicking the ball past them into the makeshift goal they'd set up near the fence.

"Goal!" he shouted, holding his arms up in victory. "GOALLL!!!"

"Your little brother's cute," Tonya said.

"Oh, he's a total character," Becky told her, rolling her eyes. "For Halloween, he's already decided he wants to be a ninja vampire cat. Who plays soccer. I know it's still more than a month away, but he likes to plan things."

Tonya giggled. "I guess he'll need the time if he's going to put all that together."

"He's got it all figured out," Becky told her. She picked up the pencil she'd been using to sketch with earlier and pulled over a piece of paper. "See, the ninja mask goes over his face with the cat ears on top of his head. Vampire teeth, obviously, and fake blood coming from the corner of his mouth. Cat tail and a cape. And he's carrying a soccer ball. Totally simple."

Tonya inspected the sketch. "Oh, *now* it all makes sense. I'm sure every person who opens the door to him will be like, 'Of course! A ninja cat vampire soccer player!' I was always just a witch or someone for trick-or-treating, and now I realize I was missing out."

"I know," Becky said. "I spent three Halloweens in elementary school dressed as a pirate, when I could have been, say, an undead pirate cheerleader rock star."

Next to Nate on the other side of the table, Robin was talking to Noah about the cheerleading squad. "Everyone knows that their coach lets the girls already on the team decide who gets to join," she said. "If they want to get treated as a sports team, they have to act like all the other sports teams, which means whoever does best in tryouts makes the squad. It's either a sport or a popularity contest, but it can't be both."

Her eyes were bright and intense with conviction behind her glasses: Anything Robin believed, she believed a hundred percent. She spread her opinions widely and often talked everyone else around to her point of view. It seemed pretty likely that the cheerleading tryouts would soon be run differently. Robin always knew everything and *told* everyone everything.

"Knowledge is power," Becky had heard her say once. "And if everybody knows what you want them to know, you can change the world." Becky wasn't sure if Robin was the world's biggest gossip or a total force for social justice.

Nate glanced toward Becky, just the barest flick of his brown eyes, but Becky wondered if he had read her mind, because he suddenly said to Robin,

"Can you believe that everyone at school was teasing Becky because she lives next to the old McNally house?"

"Because of all the ghost stories?" Robin looked outraged. "That's awful!"

Bear had been chasing the soccer ball the younger kids had kicked in the waning light. Suddenly, he lost his footing and crashed sidelong into the fence between Becky's house and the McNally house.

"Bear!" Becky called, but he was on his feet again in a second, shaking himself. Then he froze, staring at the fence. His shoulders stiffened, and the fur along his back began to bristle.

"What's wrong with Bear?" Jake asked. He and his friends had stopped moving, their game forgotten.

There was a low rumble of thunder, and Becky glanced up nervously at the sky. Black clouds had covered the sun, heavy and ominous, though it had been clear a moment before. Goose bumps rose on Becky's arms.

Then they all heard what was upsetting Bear, though it was almost inaudible at first. A throaty, pained moan was coming from the other side of the fence. Gradually, it got louder and louder, becoming a deep, mournful howl.

Becky felt the hairs at the back of her neck prickle: The sound was almost unearthly, like nothing she'd ever heard before. It didn't sound like a regular dog's howl — it was much wilder, more frightening, and sadder.

Eventually, the sound died away, trembling and wavering, becoming a moan again, and finally fading.

As it stopped, Bear snapped out of whatever had been keeping him frozen and bolted across the lawn and up the porch steps. He dove under the table, knocking an empty chair over with a *bang*. A second later, Becky felt his head land in her lap. He was whimpering softly, and she rubbed his ears comfortingly, even though she felt sick herself. *Something's wrong*, she thought anxiously. *Something's really wrong.*

Thunder cracked again from the black clouds overhead, and Danielle Kolodny began to cry. Both she and her brother ran out of the yard, heading for their own house down the street.

"What was *that*?" Tonya asked after a second, wide-eyed.

"I have no idea," Becky said helplessly. "Maybe another dog?" She didn't think so, though, not really. But what else could it have been?

Noah snorted. "A werewolf, maybe."

"I'm going to head home," Tonya said, and there was a little tremor in her voice. "It's getting late, anyway. Thanks for dinner, Becky." She got to her feet.

"I'll come with you," Noah said, and Robin got up, too.

A minute later, all three were heading down the street, away from the McNally house. Noah and Tonya were whispering to each other, their heads together, and Becky saw Robin pull out her cell phone, no doubt ready to spread the story all over school.

As they headed back to their normal houses on their normal street, Becky found herself wishing she could go with them.

Chapter Four

"Mom, you don't understand," Becky said, as her parents did the dishes. "It wasn't just a regular noise." At the table, Jake nodded, his face solemn. They'd been trying to tell their parents about the eerie howl that had come out of the McNally yard, but with one look at her mother's skeptical face Becky knew they hadn't been able to get across how very scary it had been. The kitchen was warm and brightly lit, so normal and safe that it was hard to explain just how *wrong* everything had felt outside.

"It was probably a stray cat in the yard next door," her mother said reasonably. "Let's keep an eye out, and if we see it, we can try to catch it and take it to the animal shelter."

"Bear was really scared, too," Jake said, his face stubborn. "He wouldn't be scared of a stray cat."

Their father's eyebrows rose. "Wait, Bear was there? What was Bear doing when the noise started?"

"He wasn't doing anything!" Becky said, feeling defensive. She folded her arms across her chest. Her parents exchanged a glance. She should have known that they would find a way to make this all about Bear.

"Honey," her mother said firmly, setting down a mug, "we know you love Bear, but he needs to stay off the neighbors' property. And that includes the empty house next door. If he's scaring stray animals over there, he could get hurt."

"*Mom*," Becky said indignantly, "Bear wasn't even over there. He was with us in the yard. He didn't do *anything*. Whatever it was just howled at him for no reason. And you didn't hear this noise. It wasn't any stray cat. It was, like, a banshee or something." She was breathing hard, and she realized as she said it that it was true: The sound felt too eerie to have been made by anything natural.

Her parents stared at her. Then her dad gave a little huffing sigh. "You can't just make up ridiculous stories to cover up Bear's bad behavior," he said.

Becky blinked hard and looked away from her parents. She stared instead at the big poster of different kinds of peppers that her mom had hung over the table, trying to will back tears. They were being so unfair. "Listen," she said, working to keep her voice reasonable, "you don't know all the stuff I've heard about the house next door. Everyone says it's haunted. Or that a mad scientist lived there, or . . . different things . . ."

The corners of her dad's mouth twitched as if he was stopping himself from laughing, and Becky wanted to scream.

"There's something weird about that house," she told them. "Why do you think it's been empty for so long?"

"The house next door is *haunted*?" Jake asked. He broke into a huge grin. "That's amazing!"

Becky's mom set down the sponge and turned around. "Of course it's not haunted, Jake. Becky, don't try to scare your brother. The house is empty because old Mrs. McNally lives in assisted living now, but she doesn't want to sell it or rent it out," she said matter-of-factly.

"There's always a rational explanation for

everything," Becky's father said. "Now, who wants to watch that movie I picked up?"

"I'll make popcorn," her mom said. On her way toward the pantry, she put her hands gently on Becky's shoulders. "I know that moving to a new place can be hard," she said sympathetically, "but making up stories won't help. This is a wonderful house on a terrific street, and you'll adapt."

Becky's shoulders twitched with irritation, and her mom let go. "I do love the house," Becky said, turning to look at her mom, "but there's something strange about the house next door."

"I'm sorry, Becky, but that's just not true," her mom said.

"And Becky?" her dad said, and she turned back around to look at him. He pointed one finger at her across the table. "The conversation about Bear's behavior is not over."

In bed that night, Becky couldn't get comfortable. She could hear Bear downstairs in his crate, shifting around restlessly, and occasionally letting out a soft whimper. He didn't like sleeping in the crate, but her parents insisted that he stay in the kitchen at night.

Outside, branches blew against her window. Past them, Becky watched the full moon sailing high in the sky. She buried her face in her pillow and shut her eyes. She had to get some sleep.

Downstairs, Bear barked, one sharp bark. Becky's eyes flew open again, and she listened, wondering if her parents had heard him, but there was no sound from their room. Another whimper came from downstairs, and she threw back her covers and climbed out of bed. Bear was lonely.

Becky tiptoed down the stairs without turning on the light. The moonlight coming through the windows washed across the floor, bright enough to see by.

When Bear saw her, he jumped to his feet, his tail wagging hard enough to rattle the crate.

"Shh, Bear, shh," she said softly. She knelt down on the kitchen floor and put her hands through the bars of the crate to pet him. Bear wagged his tail even harder and licked her fingers enthusiastically. "You need to go to sleep, boy," she told him in a whisper. "If you wake up Mom and Dad, they're not going to be happy with us."

As Becky started to stand up, Bear gave her a sad look, his big brown eyes wide, and her heart melted.

"Okay, honey," she whispered. "You can come with me just for tonight." Bear whuffed happily at her as she unlatched the crate. "Shh," she said, grabbing hold of his collar.

Bear followed her eagerly up the stairs, Becky wincing at the loud click of his nails against the wood. She closed her bedroom door behind them and let out a sigh of relief that her parents hadn't woken up.

Patting the rug next to her bed, she called Bear softly, but he ignored her and instead heaved himself up onto her bed, turned in a half circle to get comfortable, and stretched out.

"No, Bear," Becky whispered, trying not to laugh.

Bear gave a deep sigh of satisfaction and closed his eyes.

"Bear . . ." Becky said warningly. But he didn't move, and somehow seemed to be settling himself more firmly into the bed. He looked so smug and so set in place that, after a moment, Becky just gave up and climbed into the bed next to him. Bear immediately snuggled next to her, resting his furry head against her shoulder. Becky closed her eyes and tried again to fall asleep. She felt safer with Bear's warm, solid presence beside her.

A few minutes later, Bear began to snore. Becky's eyes snapped open. One of Bear's legs was digging into her stomach and his fur was plastered against the skin of her arm and neck, making her hot and uncomfortable. "Bear, move," she said, pushing at him, but he simply nuzzled closer in his sleep and went on snoring.

Gradually, Becky became aware of a constant, low whining noise. It occasionally stopped, but always started again. Was Bear whining in his sleep? No, his breathing was regular and steady, interspersed with soft, deep snores. The whining was coming from somewhere else.

Outside, maybe? Becky climbed out of bed. The floor was cold against her feet as she moved hesitantly toward the window, following the sound. When she looked out the window, the scene was shadowy, but lit by the full moon.

Maybe there was a stray cat or lost dog in the McNally yard, as Becky's parents had suggested. She peered down into the patch of the yard next door that she could see through her window. The whining was a little louder now, and irregular. Not the sound of the porch swing creaking or a branch rubbing against the house, but definitely some kind of animal. Becky pressed her forehead against the cold windowpane, trying to see.

Something moved in the shadows on the other side of the fence.

It was a huddled shape below one of the evergreen trees in the McNally yard. As Becky watched, it moved a little farther into the moonlight.

Was it a cat, after all? It seemed like it might be cat-size, but the shape didn't seem quite right. The tail was too short, the body looked off somehow. It was moving stiffly, not with the smooth glide of a hunting cat.

The animal raised its head and looked right at Becky. Its eyes flashed a sick, glowing yellowish green.

Instinctively, she moved back, away from the window. Had it seen her? Her heart pounded and she felt like she couldn't catch her breath. Panic bubbled inside her. She didn't know why, but she didn't want the creature to know she was there.

Suddenly, she gagged. There was a horrible smell coming from somewhere. From outside? A smell like rotting meat. It smelled like . . . death.

The smell couldn't be coming from the animal — it was just a stray in the yard next door, right? But maybe it was sick and needed help. And the flash of glowing eyes must just have been a reflection of light from somewhere, maybe of the moonlight. Steeling herself, she moved back to the window and looked out again.

It was still there, and the feeling of irrational dread in Becky's stomach increased. The animal's eyes were dark now, the shadowy head tilted back as if it was still gazing right at her window. The whining was louder, and the smell stronger. *Be brave*, Becky told herself firmly. *There's nothing to be scared of.*

Behind her, Bear sneezed suddenly, and Becky jumped and turned to look at him. He had stretched out to cover even more of the bed and was still fast asleep.

Becky turned back to the window and gazed down into the McNally yard again. She scanned the shadows and the patches of moonlit ground but, whatever the creature had been, it was gone. The smell lingered, although it seemed a little weaker now, and Becky's stomach turned over.

The animal, whatever it was, *had* seen her with its glowing eyes. Becky *knew* it on some level, even if her reason told her otherwise. Wrapping her arms around herself, she shuddered.

Chapter Five

Monday afternoon Becky sat in social studies class, barely listening to the mythology presentations by her classmates. She and Nate had already presented about the Egyptians and mummification, and things had gone pretty well. Charlotte and Lila were just finishing, and Becky only felt a tiny pang of sadness about spending so little time with Charlotte lately. Instead, her mind was taken up with a question: Should she tell someone about the weird little creature in the backyard of the McNally house?

When she had woken up Saturday morning, the panicky feeling she had gotten the previous night hadn't gone away, and she thought the sour, rotting smell lingered, too, although maybe that was just her imagination. She'd managed to sneak Bear back down to the kitchen before her parents got up, and it had been a normal rest of the weekend: no eerie howling, no creepy dreams, no one telling her scary rumors about the house next door.

But whenever she looked over at the McNally house, the little hairs on the back of her neck stood up.

The next two nights, she'd stood at her window for a long time after turning out her light. But nothing came out into the moonlit yard of the house next door and looked up at her. She lay awake for a while but didn't hear any strange whining. The horrible smell faded.

But, despite all that, Becky still felt unsettled.

Usually, if something bothered her, she'd tell Charlotte. She looked sideways to where Charlotte sat with her eyes fixed attentively on the kids who were now presenting to the class. Her hair was pulled back neatly, as usual, and she was wearing pretty dangly gold earrings. She looked put together in a way Becky just wasn't. Didn't they used to be more alike?

They'd talked on the phone on Sunday. It had been comfortable and normal for a while and then Charlotte had started telling her about something funny Lila had said in chorus, and Becky had felt left out. It seemed like Charlotte was going in a new direction, and Becky was afraid that telling Charlotte about the weird things that had been happening would just make her go in that other direction faster.

As if she felt Becky's eyes on her, Charlotte glanced over and gave her a little smile. Becky smiled back. No, she couldn't talk to Charlotte about it.

"Okay," Mr. Clauson said, breaking into Becky's thoughts. "Thank you, Alison and Katy." Everyone clapped. "Paul and Toby, you're up next."

Paul bounded up to the front of the class and unrolled a big poster that said ZOMBIES: COMMON THEMES ACROSS THE AGES. His partner, Toby, trailed after him, looking bored, and held one side of the poster. Paul pulled a stack of index cards out of his pocket.

"Zombies, or the walking dead, appear in the myths of a lot of different cultures," Paul said, his eyes shining behind his glasses. "Sometimes they're raised by necromancers or witch doctors to perform certain tasks, and sometimes they can't stay in their graves because they want something. Some want to eat brains —" At this, there were some giggles around the classroom, and Becky saw that Charlotte's face looked as if she'd eaten something rotten.

Paul continued, "Some zombies are controlled by whoever created them, and some want to bite other people to make them into zombies, too. And some just want to be put back to rest. Some are known for killing plants around them, and some cultures say they affect the weather. But they're always accompanied by a horrible smell and are usually active at night, when they can be tracked by their glowing green eyes." He stopped to shuffle through the index cards.

Becky's eyes widened and she sat up straight, her heart pounding. This had to be a coincidence. Yes, there had been the strange thunder and the bad smell and the flash of green eyes in the darkness. But there were no such things as zombies.

Were there?

In the hall after class, Becky was at her locker, trying hard not to think about zombies, when she heard Robin's voice.

"It was *unbelievably* scary," Robin was saying. She was in the center of a group of kids farther down the hall. "This awful howling noise. I don't think we should sweep this kind of thing under the rug. I told Mr. Thompson that we ought to run a feature about it in the school paper, to *warn* people, but he said that ghost stories weren't the kind of thing the paper should cover. So closed-minded."

Becky groaned inwardly. If Robin really got going, she'd probably end up hiring a team of real-life ghost-busters to exorcise Becky's neighborhood. Or, more likely, she'd talk them into showing up for free.

"You know, I heard that a coven of witches used to do rituals in that house," another voice said. Becky peeked past her locker door again and saw a sixth grade boy whose name she didn't know. He was speaking, his face self-important. "My brother told me a bunch of kids from his school were playing truth or dare, and they got dared to spend the night in that house. And they thought it was really funny, right? But then they went in one night and they *never came back out.* They were never seen again."

"That's not true," Robin said dismissively. "It would have been in the news if a whole group of high school kids disappeared."

"The police covered it up, so people wouldn't be scared to live in this town," the boy muttered. But most of the other kids in the group around them seemed to agree with Robin, and Becky felt a little better. Maybe not everyone would always believe every stupid story that was going around.

"Anyway, that house is seriously creepy," Lila chimed in. "I wouldn't live next door to it for a million dollars. Don't you think so, Charlotte?" Lila and Charlotte had walked up to the group, and Lila's face was wrinkled with disgust.

"Um . . ." Charlotte was looking over at Becky, her face sympathetic. Their eyes met, and Becky willed Charlotte to defend her. They were best friends! Even if she did think Becky's street was scary, surely she wouldn't say so to a bunch of people.

"It's a really creepy place to live, don't you think, Charlotte?" Lila said again.

Charlotte winced and looked away from Becky. "Yeah, I do," she finally answered.

Becky slammed her locker and quickly walked away, down the hall toward the buses. A minute later, she heard running footsteps behind her.

"Hey," Charlotte said breathlessly, coming up beside her.

Becky ducked her head and walked faster.

"Wait," Charlotte said. "Are you mad at me?"

Becky stopped and looked at her friend in disbelief. Charlotte's brown eyes were wide, and she looked honestly confused.

"Of course I'm mad at you!" Becky exclaimed. "You told everyone you thought my house was creepy!"

Charlotte frowned. "I said I thought it would be creepy to live next door to the McNally house," she corrected. "I didn't mean to hurt your feelings."

"Well, you did," Becky said shortly. She started walking again, heading out the doors. Charlotte followed.

"Listen," Charlotte said, reaching out to touch her arm. "Just because I think the McNally house is creepy, doesn't mean I think *you* are." Her eyes were warm, and Becky felt a little better. "Maybe we can do something next weekend?"

"Okay," Becky said as she approached her bus. "Maybe my mom can take us to the mall or something."

"Wait. Shoot," Charlotte said. "No, I forgot, I already have plans all weekend with Lila."

Becky's heart sank. "Whatever," she said. "I'll see you later." She got onto her bus and sank down in a seat. When she looked out the window, Charlotte was already climbing the stairs of her own bus.

Nate and Paul flopped down in the seat right in front of Becky. "Hi," Nate said, swiveling around. "What're you looking so sad about?"

Shrugging, Becky decided to put her bad mood behind her. "Nothing," she said, pasting on a smile. "I liked your zombie report, Paul. And, Nate, I thought the Egyptian report went really well, didn't you?"

Nate gave her a suspicious look, like he didn't believe there wasn't anything wrong, but didn't push the question. "It was pretty good. Everybody liked your drawings," he said. "Hey, do you want to hang out with me and Paul this afternoon? We're going for a walk around the neighborhood."

"Sure, why not?" Becky said. She didn't want to talk about zombies, because it was *not possible* that she might have seen one. But it would be nice to spend time with people who weren't totally obsessed with the McNally house.

* * *

Paul was *totally* obsessed with the McNally house. It turned out that *We're going for a walk around the neighborhood* was some kind of code for *Sherlock here needs to investigate the haunted house next door to you.*

Paul had carefully paced around the house as far as he could, snapping pictures of it and its yard from every angle, and even from above, through Becky's bedroom window. Jake had gotten home from school a little after they did, and he joined Nate and Becky as they followed Paul around, watching as he conducted what was clearly some kind of investigation.

"Have you ever smelled anything you couldn't explain, like maybe a rotting smell, or some sort of herbal scent, maybe?" Paul asked, standing in Becky's yard and looking thoughtfully at the fence between them and the McNally house.

"Why would I have?" Becky answered, shifting nervously from one leg to the other. She just wanted to forget the smell that had risen from the yard that weekend. Paul was freaking her out.

"Well, like I said in my report, it's a common sign of zombies," Paul said matter-of-factly, raising his camera and taking a shot of the fence.

Nate laughed.

"Zombies!" Jake exclaimed delightedly. "Awesome!" He began to lurch around the yard, arms extended. "Brains . . . brains . . ." he moaned.

Becky frowned. Now she remembered that Paul had been one of the first ones to tell stories about the McNally house, talking about a mad scientist creating monsters. "Listen," she said. "I don't think we need any more rumors about this street."

Paul adjusted his glasses and gave her a thoughtful frown. "This isn't just a rumor," he said. "My father knew Dr. McNally, and he knew what he was working on. That's one of the reasons I wanted to study zombies for my presentation."

"What are you talking about?" Becky asked. Everyone else had just said things about monsters and magic when they'd talked about the McNally house. They hadn't mentioned the people who had really lived there.

"My dad told me that Dr. McNally was a brilliant scientist," Paul explained. "He spent his life working to develop some kind of herbal compound that would help cure cancer."

"So what does that have to do with zombies?" Nate asked.

"Well," Paul said slowly, "obviously, he didn't end up curing cancer. My dad knew him through the hospital they both worked at, and he said Dr. McNally got stranger and stranger. He was convinced that what he was doing was more important than curing any disease, that he was, like, conquering death itself — that's exactly what my dad said he said. And there started being all kinds of rumors about him, like that he was bringing animals back from the dead, like squirrels and lab mice and stuff. But they came back wrong somehow, all shambling and zombified. It got so that everyone at the hospital was sort of scared of him."

A memory of the creature she'd seen in the backyard of the McNally house flashed into Becky's mind, and she swallowed nervously.

"Then what happened?" Jake asked. His eyes were bright and fascinated.

Paul shrugged. "Dr. McNally died of a heart attack. Mrs. McNally said the rumors weren't true, and eventually she moved to a nursing home. But nobody wanted to live in the house after that. I thought that, whatever he'd done, there might still be something here."

Becky's heart was beating hard. "I don't think there's anything like that here," she told him.

"Well, I got all these pictures," Paul said. "I'll look at them and see if I can find any evidence. Let me know if anything happens, okay?"

Becky nodded. "Sure, but I don't think it will," she said. Her voice sounded stiff to her own ears, and she thought Nate gave her a strange look before he turned his attention back to Paul.

"So, are you done looking for zombies?" he asked. "Because if you are, we could go play on the Wii." Paul nodded wistfully, taking one last picture of the fence outside the McNally house. "Do you want to come with us, Becky?" Nate added.

"No thanks," Becky said. She didn't feel like playing video games.

The guys left for Nate's house, and Becky started inside, telling herself fiercely that she was going to stop worrying about this. There were no zombified animals in the house next door. She had seen a stray cat, that was all.

She was already up the porch steps when she realized Jake was still standing in the yard, trying to peer through the fence between their house and the McNally house.

"Jake?" she called. "Are you coming in?"

Her little brother didn't turn around. "Jake?" she called again, uncertainly.

"Did you hear what he said?" Jake asked happily over his shoulder. "Zombies? *Awesome.*"

Chapter Six

That night, Becky dreamed she climbed the fence into the McNally yard. The yellowing lawn there sucked at Becky's feet, and she felt her shoe slip off as she struggled out of the muck. Dropping to her knees next to the sinkhole, she watched in dismay as her pink Converse sneaker disappeared into the ground.

Limping with only one shoe, she found herself climbing the porch steps up to the house. They were slippery and damp, the paint peeling in weird wet stripes, and when she got inside the house, it was all moldy. Green and white fungi sprouted from the walls and grew in thick, squishy pillowlike piles all over the floor. There was no one in sight. Becky walked farther into the house, the floor disturbingly soft under her feet.

A horrible rotting smell, worse than a Dumpster on a hot day and strangely familiar, filled the air. Becky coughed and gasped, holding her nose to try to shut it out. Everything was wet with slime, and Becky let go of her nose and clutched her hands together, frightened of touching *anything*, not wanting to get that viscous, gooey slime on her hands.

There was a footstep behind her, and Becky whipped around. In the doorway loomed a tall figure, backlit by moonlight. Becky blinked, trying to make out its face. It was gaunt and pale, and as she caught sight of its staring, glazed-over eyes, Becky lurched backward with shock.

There was blood running down the creature, and there was something else wrong. It looked like its face was shredded. Its arms extended as it reached for her, and a soft, garbled moan came out of it, as if it was trying to talk through its rotted mouth.

Becky tried to run, but she couldn't make her legs work. She pressed back against the wall, and the slime dripped down over her shoulders, sticky against her back. The creature — the *zombie*, she realized with a sickening shock — shambled toward her.

When she woke up, sweating and disoriented in the dark, the first thing Becky realized was that the rotting, stomach-turning smell from the weekend — the same smell as in her dream — had come back, filling her room. The second was that Bear, who she'd snuck into her room again because he seemed lonely and restless, was no longer pressed against her legs, no longer in the bed.

"Bear?" she whispered. There was no answering woof, no shifting of doggy paws on the floor. She dropped her hand to the rug next to her bed: Maybe Bear had gone down to where she told him to sleep for once. But there was no big, furry sleeping dog there.

Bear was gone.

From outside came a long scraping noise, like claws against the side of the house. Becky held her breath. The smell in the house was so thick it almost felt solid, hanging in the air. The scraping came again, an eerie *screech*.

Nervously, Becky climbed out of bed and sidled along the wall toward the window, trying to keep out of sight. The room was chilly and it felt late. Glancing at the clock on her bedside table, she saw that it was past one in the morning.

She peered out the window into the moonlit yard below. The McNally yard was full of shadows, and for a while she didn't see anything unusual despite straining her eyes.

Then something shifted in the shadows closest to the fence and there was a quick flash of green, an eerie color reflecting the moonlight. Becky moved closer to the window. There was a humped shape by the fence, moving up and down. The scraping noise was coming more frequently now, in time with the movement of the creature. Straining her eyes to see in the darkness, Becky tried to figure out what it was down there, and what it was doing. Too big to be a squirrel or a lab rat, whatever Paul had said. Too thin to be a raccoon, and the shape didn't seem quite right for a cat.

With a shudder, she finally realized what the creature, whatever it was, was doing. It was digging a tunnel under the fence. A tunnel into her yard.

As it began to work its way under the fence, Becky heard a whimper coming from downstairs. Her heart dropped. *Bear.*

The last thing Becky wanted to do was leave her room. It seemed so safe and cozy in comparison to the dark emptiness of the rooms downstairs right now. But the strange creature was going under the fence. What if it could manage to get into her house?

What if it attacked Bear?

She didn't believe in zombies, she told herself firmly. But whatever was out there, if it got in, even if it was only a stray animal, it could *hurt* Bear. He was just a great big puppy; he didn't know how to defend himself.

Making up her mind, Becky squared her shoulders and headed out of her room and down the hall. Bear needed her.

Going down the stairs, Becky stepped as lightly as she could and didn't turn on any lights. It seemed important not to draw attention to the fact that she was awake, or to where she was in the house. She tried to breathe slowly and evenly; her heart was pounding hard.

Down in the front hall, she stopped and listened. Was that a faint scraping noise at the front door? Could the creature have gotten under the fence so fast?

"Bear?" she whispered, padding quickly and quietly toward the kitchen. "Where are you, boy?" She could hear that her voice was shaking a little.

The faint scraping noise came again. It *definitely* was not her imagination. *What if Bear's outside?* she thought suddenly. She didn't know how he could have gotten out, but he was an escape artist, after all. He'd gotten out of the yard loads of times. Reluctantly, Becky moved toward the door. She was going to have to look outside.

The hall light suddenly flicked on, and Becky screamed.

Her mother was standing in the hall in her pajamas, one hand on the light switch. She blinked at Becky in confusion. "Beck? What are you doing? It's the middle of the night!"

"I . . . uh." Becky swallowed nervously and said, "I heard a weird noise outside." As she spoke, she heard the scraping against the door again, louder this time.

Her mom walked over and opened the front door wide. A gust of wind blew in, blowing Becky's hair back and strengthening the thick rotting smell. But there was nothing unusual outside, no creature on the doorstep.

"Ugh, what is that?" Becky's mom coughed and covered her mouth and nose. "Did something die out there?"

"I don't know," Becky said, straining to see past her into the yard. Was there something moving out in the shadows?

Her mom closed the door. "Let's get back to bed," she said firmly. "We'll figure out the smell in the morning, if it's still there."

Bear chose that moment to wander into the hall, the tags on his collar clinking against each other and his toenails clicking on the floor. When he saw Becky, he sped up and ran toward her, a happy doggy grin stretching his mouth wide.

"Bear!" Becky's mom shouted.

Startled, Bear lost his balance, his paws skidding on the hardwood floor, and lurched into Becky, who sat down hard. Immediately, she found herself with a lap full of concerned dog. Bear pushed his cold, wet nose into her face and, realizing she was fine, licked her with his warm, even wetter tongue.

"Crazy dog," Becky said affectionately, putting her arms around him. Looking up, she saw her mom frowning.

"What is Bear doing out of his cage?" her mom asked. Her voice was angry.

"Uh . . ." Becky said, the scraping outside and the gross smell forgotten.

"Becky, you know Bear's supposed to sleep in his crate," her mom told her. Her mouth was pressed into a thin line, and she ran her hands through her hair distractedly. "If you keep encouraging him to break the rules, he's never going to learn to behave."

"I'm sorry, Mom," Becky said. She pushed Bear off her lap and got up. Sensing the tension in the air, Bear looked worriedly from Becky to her mother and whined softly.

Becky's mother sighed. "Put Bear in his crate and go to bed," she said, more gently. "But we're going to have a talk about this tomorrow."

Becky nodded and led Bear into the kitchen. He gave a small *woof* of discontent when she steered him into the crate, but he didn't fight her. He settled down on his cushion and rested his head on his big paws.

"Good night, my good boy," Becky said, stroking his ears through the bars. "Sweet dreams." Bear, his eyes already drifting closed, nuzzled her fingers, then thumped his tail once against the floor.

Becky's mom had already gone upstairs. Becky flicked off the hall light and was about to follow her when, once more, she heard a slow scrape against the front door, as if something was asking to come in.

Shivering, she hurried up the stairs. She tried to make herself believe she was imagining the sound and that, if there had been some creature digging its way under the McNally fence that night, it had been a stray cat or wild raccoon going about its private business.

There was no way it could have been a zombie.

Chapter Seven

The next morning, Becky sat at the breakfast table with dry eyes and a pounding headache. It had taken her a long time to fall asleep after shutting Bear in his crate, and it felt like almost no time had passed before her alarm went off and she had to get up again. She poked disinterestedly at her cereal.

The rotting smell was weaker but still lingering, and it was making her feel sick at the thought of eating anything.

"What's up with you?" Jake asked, staring at her. "You look like you're about to fall off your chair." Without waiting for an answer, he went on, "Hey, did you tell Mom and Dad about the zombies?"

"*Zombies?*" her mom asked, sounding highly

amused. Becky tuned out her little brother's explanation of what Paul had told them. Her mom looked like she was having trouble not laughing; she clearly wasn't going to take seriously any suggestion that there might be some kind of monster next door.

Becky's dad had gone outside to call Bear in from the yard. He reappeared at the door, frowning, and called to Becky. "Come out here. I want you to see something." Becky groaned and got to her feet. She was just so sleepy.

Outside, Bear galloped over and pressed lovingly against her side. Becky's dad led her into the yard and pointed silently at a yellowed, dying patch of grass.

"Huh, weird," Becky said, not sure why her dad was showing it to her. "It wasn't like this yesterday."

Looking at the grass, she realized the patch led from the fence between their house and the McNally house, across the lawn, and toward their front door. In fact, it wasn't so much a patch as a *trail*. A trail that seemed to begin about where she had seen the creature tunneling under the fence last night.

Below the fence, just where the dead grass began, was a space, one that might have been scraped out by paws. Becky gasped, remembering what Paul had said about plants dying around zombies. The creature *had* been scratching at their front door last night.

"Look," her dad said accusingly. "Look what Bear's done now."

Becky stared at him. "Bear didn't do this," she said.

Her dad spread his arms wide, indicating the spread of yellowed grass. "Honey, look around," he said. "The grass is dead where that dog goes, over and over again, pacing between the fence and the front walk. I'm sure he doesn't mean to, but he's just destructive. This is exactly why I didn't want to get a dog."

Becky stared sadly at the dead grass. Then she saw something move. She bent closer, but pulled back in disgust. A big black beetle crawled across the dirt beneath the grass. Beside it, worms squirmed past the stalks. All through the patchy grass, insects and worms twined together, thick and revolting, covering the entire path below the yellowed, patchy grass. Bear snuffled next to her, then pulled back, snorting.

"Dad . . ." Becky said, wanting to point out the squirming insects, but her father wasn't looking at the grass anymore. He was staring straight at her, his face heavy with concern.

"Becky, if you can't figure out how to keep your dog under control," he said, "we can't keep him."

Her dad's words echoed in Becky's ears all morning, making her anxious and snappy. She had trouble paying attention in her classes, and her English teacher yelled at her for spacing out during second period. By the time she got to the library for study hall, where she tripped on the carpet coming in, Becky felt like she was going to cry. *Worst day ever*, she thought. Usually, she would have sat with Charlotte, Lila, and Tonya, but she couldn't talk to them about the weird things happening at her house. Today she just wanted to talk to Nate. He was smart, and he lived on her street, so the McNally house was his problem, too. And he liked Bear.

"There's something weird going on," she told him bleakly, dropping her books on the table next to him. "I need you to help me."

Nate pushed his long bangs out of his eyes and frowned at her with concern. "What's wrong?" he asked.

Becky told him everything, feeling a tightness release in her chest just by being able to let it all out: everything from first seeing the animal in the yard next door, to its flashing green eyes, to just how *wrong* it had felt. About the creature tunneling under the fence, and about the bugs and worms wriggling through the dead grass where it had walked. Worst of all, about her dad's threat to get rid of Bear.

"They always blame everything on him," she said, her eyes filling with hot tears. "It's not fair. He's a good dog. He is."

"I know he is," Nate said. He stared at her for a minute and then said slowly, "You think Paul's story about the mad scientist and the zombies is for real?"

Becky shrugged helplessly. "It sounds crazy, but it's starting to *feel* real, you know? I just want to figure out what's going on."

Nate tapped his pencil against his lips thoughtfully. "So, what do we know about zombies?" he asked.

Relaxing suddenly, Becky let out a breath. These were crazy things she had been saying, she knew, and she realized that if Nate hadn't believed her, hadn't accepted that there was *something* going on, she wouldn't have known who else to turn to.

"Well," she said, opening her notebook, "the whole brains thing, right?" She glanced up and held her arms up stiffly in front of her for a second, letting her eyes go wide and vacant. "Braaaains, like in the movies. Only Paul said that wasn't always true, not in all the stories."

"Right," Nate said. "And getting bitten by a zombie turns you into a zombie. That's in movies, too. Only Paul said *that* wasn't always true, too."

Becky shivered. "But what if it is?" she said, panicked. "What if the creature bites someone? It might turn the animals around our house into zombies, or Bear. Bear's always roaming around! Or someone on the street. If getting bitten turns you into one, then no one is safe!"

Mrs. DaCosta, the librarian, shushed her from her desk, frowning, and Becky realized her voice had risen. Glancing hurriedly around, she saw a couple of kids staring at them from the nearby tables.

"Take a deep breath," Nate said. "But you're right — we need to assume that the bite of a zombie *can* turn you into a zombie, since there's no way to prove that it doesn't. That makes this a dangerous situation. So if we figure out how to get rid of the zombie, we can keep everyone safe." He huffed out a quiet laugh, his hair falling back into his eyes. "This is the craziest conversation."

"You believe me about the thing in the yard, though, right?" Becky asked.

Nate looked straight at her, his blue eyes shining with sincerity through his shaggy bangs. "Of course I do," he said simply, and Becky felt better. "Let's make a list of everything we remember from Paul's report," he said, and she looked back down at her notebook.

She started writing.

1) *Some zombies eat brains.*
2) *The bite of a zombie could turn you into a zombie.*
3) *Bad smell comes with zombies.*
4) *Zombies are active at night.*
5) *They have glowing eyes.*

"They come because they want something, or someone calls them," Nate added, and Becky wrote:

6) *Exist because they are either called or they want something.*

"What else?" she asked.

"What did Paul say?" Nate said, remembering. "That Dr. McNally made zombie animals when he was trying to use herbs to cure cancer, right?"

Becky wrote:

7) Made by herbal medicine?

"Anything else?" she asked.

Nate shrugged. "I don't know a lot about monsters," he said. "Do we want to ask Paul more about this? He's obviously the expert."

Becky shook her head. "I'd like to keep this kind of quiet," she said. She couldn't help remembering the looks of disgust and pity on Lila's and Charlotte's faces when they had called her house creepy. "And I'm sure he put everything he knew into his report."

"Let's try looking online, then," Nate said. "We're supposed to use library period for doing research, anyway, right?"

Becky followed him to an empty terminal and pulled up a second chair. Nate typed *zombies* into the browser's search bar. Then he gave a low whistle.

"There are a *lot* of computer games about zombies," he said. "And movies. I'm not seeing much real information here."

"Try *herbal cause for zombies*," Becky suggested. Nate typed it in.

"Huh," he said. "Here's some stuff from the Voodoo Museum in New Orleans." They both leaned forward to read. This website described several different kinds of zombies: spiritual zombies, which were reanimated corpses; bargained zombies, where people offered to let the voodoo master take their souls in return for protection; and, lastly, herbal zombies.

"Herbal zombies — that sounds like what Paul was talking about," Nate murmured. "Ew, through their feet."

The website said that voodoo practitioners would first poison their victims with a paralyzing nerve poison that came from blowfish, which they would secretly put in their targets' shoes to be absorbed by the sweat glands in the feet.

"Yikes," said Becky. "I hope that's not what Dr. McNally did to the lab rats."

She wrote down the facts in her notebook, anyway, under the heading *Voodoo Zombies*. Looking at her neat list of the information they had so far, she felt a little pang for the study sessions she'd shared with Charlotte last year; Charlotte had always complained that Becky needed to make organized lists and outlines to study efficiently.

"Let's try another search," she said, typing in *getting rid of zombies*. They scanned the results. "Yuck, I am *not* cutting off anything's head."

Unfortunately, any real information about zombies was buried among a ton more sites about games and movies and books. After a while, they found a little more advice that looked relevant on a website that seemed to be mostly about magic.

"It says here that a paste made of poppy seeds and cloves can help put a zombie to rest," Becky said, her eyes taking in the words onscreen. "And it says that if it's the kind of zombie that wants something before it goes away, it can't be put to rest until it gets what it's looking for. Like, if it lost something important to it."

"It was some kind of animal, though, right?" Nate said. "What could it be looking for? Was it a squirrel?" He crossed his eyes at her, then held his arms up in front of him in a zombie pose. "Aaaaacorns," he said. "Aaaaacorns."

"What're you guys doing?" Charlotte's voice said behind them, and Becky turned toward her. Charlotte was smiling and looked like she was about to start laughing at Nate's zombie squirrel impression. But then her eyes fell on the computer screen in front of them and she frowned instead. Becky glanced over to see what Charlotte was looking at.

On the computer screen a gray-skinned monster, flesh stripping off its bones, lurched toward the viewer, its mouth open in a moan. Above it flashed in glaring red letters *"ZOMBIE DEATH RACE: RUN, DEAD MEN, RUN!"* Becky felt her face start to heat up.

"It's a role-playing game," Nate said smoothly. "I've been trying to get Becky into it."

Charlotte looked at Becky's neat list of things like *some zombies eat brains* and *the bite of a zombie could turn you into a zombie* and made a face, her nose wrinkling in disgust. "You guys are so weird," she said. "I'll talk to you later, Becky."

They both watched as she crossed the library back to the table where Lila and Tonya sat and said something to them. Lila glanced over at them and laughed.

"If we don't get rid of this zombie, not only am I

going to lose my dog, I'm going to have no friends left at all," Becky said glumly.

Nate nudged her with his elbow, his face sympathetic. "You'll still have *me*," he said, and Becky, feeling warmed, nudged him back.

Chapter Eight

Nate came over that afternoon to inspect the damage the zombie (or whatever the creature was) had done to the yard.

"Jeez, it stinks," he said, clapping one hand over his nose and mouth.

"You should have smelled it last night," Becky told him. "It was even worse." The smell now was more a background nastiness rather than the heavy, suffocating stink it had been before. She led him into the backyard, where they looked at the path of dead grass. Below the yellowed blades of grass, worms and insects still wriggled and squirmed. Becky backed away in disgust as a long pink worm writhed toward her, moving quickly and jerkily.

"Yeah, I really don't think this is a natural thing," Nate said, looking pale and slightly nauseous.

When they went inside, they found Becky's mom in the kitchen, scrubbing out the inside of the cabinet under the sink. She looked flustered and hot, her hair sticking out frizzily. She straightened up when she saw them, pulling off her rubber gloves and tossing them in the sink.

"I've been cleaning all day," she said tiredly. "I just can't figure out where that smell is coming from. I don't think it's the pipes. Do you think Bear brought a dead squirrel or something in here, Becky?"

"No!" Becky said indignantly. "Why are you and Dad always blaming everything on Bear?"

Her mom gave her a sudden sympathetic smile. "Poor Bear," she said. "I know he doesn't mean to make trouble, honey. But he gets into so many messes that we've gotten into the habit of thinking he's probably behind anything that goes wrong."

"I think the smell's coming from outside, Mrs. Nolan," Nate said politely. "Maybe somebody's using a pesticide on the trees or something?"

"Maybe," Becky's mom said doubtfully. "I'll have to talk to the neighbors." She ran her hands through her hair, making it frizz a little more. "I'll call around and see if anyone knows what's causing the stink." She plucked her phone off the counter and was already dialing as she left the kitchen.

Becky led Nate back out into the backyard, and they circled the house, looking for clues. Jake was crouched by the driveway, poking the squirming insects in the grass with a stick.

"Isn't this cool?" he asked.

Becky shook her head. "You like such gross things," she said, and Jake laughed.

Becky pulled Nate over by the fence, out of Jake's earshot. "You know we need to go next door if we're going to find anything out," she said unhappily. Her hands were sweaty.

There was a long, taut pause. They both looked at the high wooden fence in front of them and the bit of the McNally house they could glimpse behind it.

"Yeah, you're right," Nate said. He gave her a small smile. "It's daytime, though — the zombie won't be out." Becky tried to smile back and look reassured, even though her stomach was flip-flopping wildly.

The board in the corner of the fence was still loose, and it screeched loudly as Becky pushed it back. She glanced nervously toward Jake, but he seemed oblivious, dangling a worm from the end of his stick. Her own house was still and quiet, sunlight reflecting peacefully off the windows. In contrast, the McNally yard looked shadowed and ominous, and Becky really wished for a moment that Jake would look up and ask what they were doing, or that her mom would come bursting out and stop them.

No one came, though, and Becky led the way into the yard of the McNally house.

It wasn't immediately scary, just quiet and still. The hole behind the loose board let them out into the space between a couple of evergreen trees. Becky had to push branches out of her way to move forward, holding them back so they didn't hit Nate behind her.

The yard between the fence and the McNally house was a maze of dead and dying yellow grass, multiple wandering trails leading from one to the other, as if something had paced back and forth from the house to the fence. One trail led directly to the dark hole dug beneath the fence and into Becky's yard. Becky walked closer and peered at the nearest patch of dead grass and below it, as she'd expected, saw the sinuous writhing mass of black beetles and pink worms, moving slowly along the trail.

"Just like at your house," Nate said thoughtfully, coming up beside her. "Maybe you should show your parents, so they know Bear wasn't the one who made the grass die."

"I don't think that'll work," Becky told him. "First of all, we're *trespassing*, remember? I don't think we should give them evidence. And they'd just say Bear's been sneaking in here, anyway, and he'd get in more trouble."

"I didn't think of that," Nate said, his shoulders drooping. He looked so disappointed that Becky felt bad.

"Thanks for trying to get Bear out of trouble, though," she said. Nate shook his hair out of his eyes and smiled at her again. She jostled her shoulder against his lightly, glad that he was with her.

Stepping cautiously over the trails of yellowed grass, they walked away from the corner where they'd come into the yard. Becky was very conscious of the fact that they were getting farther and farther away from the easiest way to get back home. The house loomed above them.

Close up, she could see how it was a lot like her own house, if her house had been neglected for years. A porch swing that was a twin of the one at her house dangled from one rusty chain at one end of the wide porch. The white paint on the house and the black paint on the shutters was peeling away in long, ragged curls; the boards over the windows were weathered and dirty. There was a wide patch of mud in front of them, and Becky stepped over it nervously, remembering the sinkhole in her dream and how she'd watched her sneaker disappear, sucked underground.

From behind them came a *screech* of metal, and Becky shrieked.

"What *was* that?" she asked, grabbing Nate's arm.

"I don't know," he said nervously, glancing around. "But I feel like something's watching us." They stood still and listened, but everything was quiet.

After a few moments, Nate shrugged. "I don't think —" he began, and suddenly, something burst out of the thick evergreens by the fence.

"BOO!" Jake yelled, and Nate and Becky both screamed. Jake collapsed into giggles. "Come on," he said, leaning forward with his hands on his knees and catching his breath. "Did you guys think I couldn't see you sneaking over here? You are *so* un-ninjalike." He straightened up, and looked curious. "So what are we doing? Are we going to try to get into the house?"

"No," Becky said automatically. She *really* didn't want to go into the house. She realized that the smell was much stronger here. It made her think of disease and rotting things. She remembered the sickening give of the wet fungus under her feet in her dream, and for a moment she felt overwhelmed by dizziness.

"Jake, you should go home," she said. "It's not safe here."

Her brother snorted. "No way!" he exclaimed. "You don't get to have all the fun."

Behind them, something rustled.

Becky whipped around. There was something moving back there, she was sure of it, shaking the line of bushes between them and the side of the house. One bush had withered, orange, bell-shaped flowers hanging from it, and several fell to the ground as its branches shook.

"It's probably just a squirrel or something," Nate said nervously.

"A *zombie* squirrel, thanks to Dr. McNally," Becky muttered, and Jake giggled delightedly.

"Come on!" Jake said, and rushed in front of them. Before Becky could call him back, he'd disappeared around the corner of the house. Becky wanted to hurry after him, but somehow it seemed important not to run, almost as if running might inspire something to chase them.

Nate seemed to feel the same way. He grabbed hold of her arm, and they hopped and stepped their way over the trails of dead grass and insects, across the side yard and around the corner, calling "Jake! Wait!" Becky's heart was pounding — she couldn't hear Jake anymore.

Jake was there, bent over to peer intently into an unboarded basement window. "Hey, you guys," he said. "Check it out."

"Jake!" Becky scolded, her voice sharp with irritation. "Don't run off without us like that."

Jake shrugged. "Sorry," he said casually. "I just wanted to see what was over here."

"Well, you need to be careful, dummy," Becky said nastily.

Jake folded his arms, hugging himself defensively. His sharp white elbows stuck out, and he looked really young. Becky felt a little guilty for yelling at him. "We were worried about you," she said in a nicer voice, and Jake relaxed, letting his arms hang free.

"I'm sorry," he said again, more genuinely this time. "But look, you can see into the basement from here."

Becky and Nate both leaned forward to look through the window, squinting to adjust their eyes to the dimness below.

The basement was full of stuff — shadowy shapes stretching away into the darkness, beyond where the sunlight reached. Becky saw what looked like an old-fashioned sewing machine, a big chair covered with a sheet, and, farther back, a complicated mass of . . . something. Light glinted off the surface of whatever it was.

"It's science stuff!" Jake said excitedly. "Paul was telling the truth!"

Blinking, Becky made out the shapes of beakers, test tubes, and flasks connected by long twists of tubing. It did look like something that a mad scientist might have handy, but . . . "I'm not sure a chemistry set in the basement proves that Dr. McNally was making zombies," she said.

Jake had just opened his mouth to reply when the bushes beside the house began shaking violently again. Whatever was back there was coming closer to them, and coming fast.

Something big and dark burst from the bushes, and all three of them screamed. Jake grabbed Becky's arm, and she felt her heart race. Becky saw Nate's eyes fly wide open, the whites showing all around the irises, as he jumped backward.

A second later, they realized the angry animal bearing down on them was Bear.

But it was a Bear that Becky had never seen before. His lips were drawn back in a snarl, and his teeth looked huge and sharp. His ears were pressed down flat, and his eyes were bright and focused on them, as if the three of them were the only things he could see. And he was charging toward them so fast that all they could do, without even thinking about it, was run.

Becky could hear the harsh pants behind them as Bear chased them all around the house, almost close enough to nip at their legs. She ran blindly, taking no time to avoid the trails of dead grass. *Did the zombie get him?* she thought. *Oh no, oh no, oh, Bear.*

Becky felt a crunch underfoot and winced as she realized she might have just ground a bunch of beetles beneath her sneaker. She felt a squish of mud as she ran over the place she had thought might be a sinkhole. She was sweating and short of breath, a sharp pain in her side. Finally, they were at the loose board again, and Becky held it back as she shoved her little brother through it in front of her.

Jake was crying — big, deep sobs — and Becky pushed him in front of them as they all ran toward the house. As they reached the porch steps, she turned back and suddenly stopped, Jake and Nate pausing beside her.

Bear had finished pulling himself out from under the fence, and all the rage seemed to have gone out of him. He ducked his head and wagged his tail low and uncertainly, every line of his body expressing shame and worry. He whimpered appealingly.

A realization came crashing over Becky, driving out all the fear. Bear hadn't been angry or trying to hurt them. "Bear was trying to protect us," she said. "He was herding us away from where he thought there was danger."

Jake sniffed. "Really?" he said hopefully. Nate tilted his head a little and looked at Bear thoughtfully.

Becky nodded. "Look at him," she said. She held out her hand, and Bear gave a great doggy grin of joy at being forgiven. He galloped toward them. When he reached them, he licked indiscriminately at their hands and legs, his tail beating hard.

"You can't tell Mom and Dad that Bear chased us," Becky told Jake fiercely. "They're already mad at him, and they said they'd get rid of him if he made more trouble."

Jake stroked Bear's head. "I know," he said, sniffling. "I won't say anything." His voice shook a little. "But why did Bear think he needed to protect us? Is there really a zombie?"

Nate swallowed. "Whatever it is," he said thoughtfully, "*something* is really freaking Bear out."

"I don't want to play zombies anymore," Jake said, and kicked at the grass.

Becky looked nervously at the fence between the houses. She really didn't want to think about the *something* that might have scared Bear so much that the dog had chased them out of the yard. The tops of the trees above the fence were moving gently in the breeze, and the afternoon seemed calm. But something was over there — something dangerous. And Bear knew it.

Chapter Nine

By dinnertime, Becky was a mess. She couldn't stop remembering the horrible moment when she had been convinced that the zombie had bitten Bear, that he was a zombie, too. That her darling, sweet dog had become a monster, and that he was after her. Just the thought of it made Becky's chest feel hollow and her eyes sting.

And what if the zombie had been right there, lurking in the bushes? They didn't really know that zombies only came out at night. It wasn't just Bear. They were all in danger. If the zombie was real — and, even though it was almost impossible to believe, a deep-inside part of Becky was sure it was true — any of them could be bitten and turned into a zombie as well. Her mom and dad, Jake, Nate, Becky herself, all the neighbors, any of them could be attacked. Becky swallowed. She and Nate were the only ones who knew.

It was trash night, and when Becky wheeled out the recycling bin, a light, dismal rain was falling and thunder rumbled in the distance. Dragging the cans to the curb, Becky glanced up at the sky and then looked nervously around. Was the zombie causing this weather?

Becky frowned, a thought niggling at the back of her mind. She remembered thunder crashing the week before as she pulled Bear into the house, and again, out of a sky that had been blue a second before, when Bear ran into the fence between their house and the house next door.

It was almost like the zombie was angry with Bear.

But why would it be? What could *Bear* have done to upset a zombie?

As she dragged the can the rest of the way to the curb, Becky was thinking so hard that she was barely aware of how much stronger the rotting smell that had hung around all day was getting. When she reached the curb, though, it flooded her senses so much that she had to let go of the can to cough and cover her face with her hands. It was heavy and foul, even worse than it had been the night before.

Suddenly, from the sidewalk beside her came a thick, wet-sounding snarl.

A small animal was coming toward her slowly, its green eyes shining unnaturally in the glow from the streetlights. She realized that it was dragging its left hind leg behind it, moving painfully. Becky froze as the creature came closer to her, stepping into the light.

Then she blinked in shock. It was a Chihuahua.

But not a normal Chihuahua. As it came closer still, its flashing green eyes fixed on her, Becky saw that its fur was matted and full of dirt. One ear hung off at a funny angle, seeming to be attached only by a long strip of ragged flesh. It crept toward her, its small body vibrating with that same curiously wet snarl. The smell got even worse, and Becky gagged and stumbled backward.

Becky was sure, beyond a shadow of a doubt, that this was a zombie Chihuahua. She gasped a high gasp that was almost a scream and ran for the house. *It's real*, she thought dizzily. *There's really a zombie!*

The rain was harder now, pattering down on her head and shoulders.

It's coming after me, she realized with a thrill of horror, looking back over her shoulder. Despite its limp, the strange little dog was moving fast, the distance between them shrinking. Its snarl was steady, without it seeming to have to pause for breath. The smell kept getting worse and worse, too, the closer the little dog got. Becky was panting and shaking, tears coming down her face, and the little dog was still snarling, its lips drawn back from its teeth, looking ready to bite.

Her shoes were pounding hard up the driveway, and the lights of her house had never seemed more welcoming. She had almost reached the porch when she tripped over her own feet and plummeted forward, landing hard, the breath knocked out of her, her hands scraping against the wet concrete.

Ignoring the stinging in her palms, Becky flipped over to look behind her through the rain, crawling crablike on her back to get her feet under herself again. Her clothes were wet and clung to her clammily.

The zombie dog was still coming at her. Now that she was on the ground, it had slowed down again and was pacing toward her with that slow limping stride, its eyes flashing greenly, the thick snarl getting louder and louder. It snapped its sharp teeth at her.

I can't let it bite me! Becky thought desperately. She didn't want to be a zombie!

Something rattled in the dog's throat, and she felt its cold breath on her leg. Becky screamed, a loud, drawn-out scream, and scrabbled desperately at the muddy ground with her hands, pulling herself away. She couldn't get up, not fast enough.

There was something hard under her hand and she grabbed it and thrust it toward the dog. It was a stick, she realized.

The Chihuahua's teeth fastened on the stick and it held on as she tried to jerk it away. For a nightmarish moment, it was almost like playing a game of tug-of-war with Bear, except that the Chihuahua's eerie green eyes were fixed steadily on her with what seemed to be a cold anger.

Pulling hard, Becky managed to yank the stick from the Chihuahua's mouth. A slow trickle of what seemed to be black blood ran from the creature's lip as it crouched down, ready to leap at her. Panicking, Becky flung the stick at it.

She missed. The zombie Chihuahua turned its head to watch the stick fly past. But then, very slowly, without looking at her again, it turned and ambled after it.

Becky leaped to her feet and ran straight to her house. She fumbled at the doorknob for a minute, her hands sweaty and scraped, then made it inside and slammed the door behind her.

Did it . . . chase the stick? she thought disbelievingly, and gave a half snort of amazed laughter. *I guess even a zombie dog is still a dog. . . .*

The sheer craziness of that thought, of the whole situation, hit her, and she closed her eyes for a moment, her head pounding.

"Becky?" her mom called from upstairs. "Are you okay? I thought I heard you yell."

Becky drew in a breath, her mind whirling. Should she tell her mom what had happened? Would her mom believe her? She couldn't imagine the conversation. "I'm fine, Mom," she called back. "I thought I saw something in the bushes, that's all."

"Okay," her mom said. "Don't forget to lock up."

Becky locked the door and then went to one of the front windows. Cautiously, she pulled the curtain aside and looked out. The porch and front steps were empty, but beyond the small circle made by the porch light, the yard was dark.

Becky wondered if the zombie dog was still out there, watching the house. Waiting.

Chapter Ten

There was no way, of course, that her parents would ever believe Becky had seen a zombie dog in the driveway the night before. She'd been worrying about how to warn her family, though: She had to let them know there was something out there to be scared of.

All the time she was letting Bear out and then feeding him and filling his water dish, Becky thought about what to say. Bear, anxious, padded around after her, his tail drooping. She wondered if he was being affected by her mood, or if he was scared of the zombie dog, too. When she sat down at the breakfast table, he collapsed at her feet, resting his head on top of her shoe, instead of begging for bacon as usual.

"Uh . . ." She cleared her throat so that her mom and dad and Jake all looked up. "Last night, I saw something outside. There was this weird little dog, and it sort of tried to bite me. I think maybe it was sick."

Her parents reacted the way she'd hoped they would. Her mom promised to call animal control and scolded Becky for not telling her the night before. Her dad made Jake promise to stay inside after school and told everyone not to let Bear wander around loose.

"Maybe Bear's been acting so strange because he knew about the stray dog," Becky suggested hopefully.

Her parents exchanged a glance, and her father put down his fork. "We've never said Bear wasn't a good dog, honey," he said. "But his behavior needs to improve, and your mom and I will have to see that you're working toward that."

Becky bit her lip and stared down at her plate. There was plenty of breakfast left, but she wasn't hungry anymore. She remembered what her dad had said out in the backyard the other day. If she couldn't keep him under control, her parents would get rid of Bear.

As if he could hear her thoughts, Bear stirred and whimpered at her feet. Poor Bear. The zombie was making him a nervous wreck, and he was getting blamed for stuff — like the destruction of the lawn — that wasn't even his fault. Becky sat up straighter as she filled with new resolve: She would get rid of the zombie, no matter what. Not only was that the best way to protect everyone, it might be the only way to save Bear.

"A Chihuahua?" Nate asked her in study hall, stifling his laugh with a fist as Mrs. DaCosta looked at him suspiciously. "Are you serious?"

"It's not funny," Becky said.

"Okay, but it's not the most threatening zombie animal I can imagine," he said, still grinning.

"Nate!" Becky said sharply. Mrs. DaCosta looked up again, and Becky quickly busied herself with her notebook and pen, pretending to work on her social studies essay. She glanced over at Charlotte sitting at another table with Lila and lowered her voice. "Did you know little dogs are more likely to bite than big dogs?" she whispered quietly with her eyes still on her paper. "I looked it up. Dachshunds are the breed of dog that bites the most often, followed by *Chihuahuas*. If a zombie's bite turns you into a zombie, it doesn't matter how big the dog is. Everyone on our street is in danger."

Nate didn't say anything for a moment, and, looking up from her notebook, Becky saw that his face was serious now.

"Okay," he said, nodding. "You're right. But there has to be a reason this dog has shown up only now. I've lived on our street all my life, and this has never happened before. We need to figure out why the zombie is here, and what we have to do to stop it. And we need to do it now."

They decided that the best way to find out what the zombie dog was doing there was to find out more about the McNallys. Nate's parents had lived on Tulip Street for years and years, since way before Nate was born. So they headed to Nate's house after school.

Becky didn't want to leave Bear alone in the backyard, where the zombie dog might get him, or in the house, where he might misbehave in front of her mother. So she snapped his leash on and brought him with them.

"Bear's not acting normal, is he?" Nate said with a worried look at the dog. Bear usually pulled the leash every which way so that he could sniff everything in his path and tangled it in front of Becky's feet. Now, though, he was sticking close by her side, his head down and his tail tucked nervously between his legs.

"He's not," Becky said, and stroked Bear's head. "That's another reason we need to figure out how to get rid of the zombie."

Nate's house was warm and sunny. His mom greeted Becky kindly and made a big fuss over Bear, petting him and saying how gorgeous he was. She also knew all about the McNallys.

"They were still living here when Nate's dad and I first moved in," she said. "The house was as nice as the other houses on this street then, and they always used to walk around the neighborhood with their two little dogs. Dr. McNally was really quiet, but Mrs. McNally loved to talk, and she was crazy about those dogs."

Becky and Nate snuck a glance at each other.

"What kind of dogs did they have?" Becky asked, trying to sound casual.

"Chihuahuas, I think," Nate's mom said. "Little yappy ones." Becky felt a chill down her spine.

Nate's mom rubbed Bear's ears, and he leaned against her leg happily. "I like big dogs like you better," she told him.

"What happened to the McNallys?" Nate asked.

His mom gave him a funny look. "Why are you so interested in Dr. and Mrs. McNally all of a sudden?" she asked. "This was all before you were born, and you've never wanted to know about them before."

Don't tell her about the zombie, Becky willed. Nate's mom was grinning at him as if she suspected he was up to something, and Nate didn't seem like he'd be a very good liar. But if he mentioned the zombie dog, his mom was just going to think they were crazy.

Nate shrugged. "Now that Becky lives next door to the McNally house, it's freaking her out," he told his mom. "Everybody tells ghost stories about it."

"Oh!" Nate's mom patted Becky's arm sympathetically. "I guess the house does look a little spooky now," she said. "But don't worry, there's nothing mysterious about it. Dr. McNally got sick and died in the hospital, and Mrs. McNally moved to that assisted living center over by the mall, Vantage Place. I'm sure she can't keep dogs over there, but those little Chihuahuas must have passed on a while back."

Finally, Becky thought, nudging Nate hard in the side. *Real evidence that connects the McNallys with the Chihuahua! I bet Mrs. McNally will be able to tell us exactly what's going on.*

Before Becky left Nate's, they made plans to head over to Vantage Place the next afternoon to visit Mrs. McNally. It would be better to talk to her face-to-face, they decided, than to call.

"We'll get visual cues from her," Nate said wisely. "Even if she doesn't tell us anything, we'll pick up more if we can see her reaction to our questions."

"And," Becky added, "if we don't call first, she can't tell us not to come over."

At home, Becky arranged for Jake to walk Bear after school the next day and told her mom that she was going to the assisted living center for a school assignment. She thought it best not to bring up the McNally house to her parents in this case.

The next afternoon, Becky and Nate caught a bus from a stop near the school.

They had to sign in at a security desk by the front door of Vantage Place. But no one asked if they had permission to visit or gave them any problem about telling them where Mrs. McNally's room was. Becky had been nervous about going and had pictured a building full of old people lying in hospital rooms, but instead the retirement home seemed very active and cheerful. They walked through a small library area, past a sitting room where a group was working on sewing projects, and caught the elevator next to a room full of exercise equipment.

Mrs. McNally lived on the fourth floor. When they got off the elevator, Becky and Nate found them-selves in a long, carpeted hallway that ran past apartment doors.

Many of the doors had little framed pictures on them: old wedding photos; big happy groups at family gatherings; pictures of smiling children. Apartment 414, Mrs. McNally's home, was a little different.

"Yikes," said Nate, staring at the door and push-ing his long hair out of his eyes to get a better look. "I guess this is the place, all right."

The picture on Mrs. McNally's door was huge — a shiny, laminated poster stretching almost the whole length of the door. On it, two brown and white Chihuahuas, larger than life-size, sat staring out at them, their mouths open to pant, their ears perked, their eyes bright, and their fur glossy. One wore a red collar, the other a blue. A red ball sat at the feet of one, a blue ball at the feet of the other.

They were cute dogs, even though their oversize appearance was slightly alarming, Becky thought. At least, she would have thought so — if she wasn't a hundred percent sure that the dog on the left, the one in a blue collar, was now the frightening and bedraggled zombie dog that had attacked her just a couple of nights before.

Chapter Eleven

Mrs. McNally turned out to be a small, straight-backed old lady with neat white hair. When she opened the door, Becky launched into the story they'd agreed on.

"Hi," she said. "We go to Lincoln Middle School, and we're doing a report on local history based on, um, houses in the area? We live on Tulip Street, I live next door to your old house, and we wanted to ask you about it?"

Mrs. McNally frowned at them thoughtfully and hesitated, then opened the door more widely. "I suppose you should come in, then," she said.

The apartment was small but bright and clean. It was also completely filled with dog stuff. *Chihuahua* stuff. On the walls there were china plates with paintings of Chihuahuas chasing balls or rolling over to have their tummies scratched. Little Chihuahua figurines sat and lay and posed on the bookshelves around the room. There was a big cross-stitch picture of a Chihuahua with a blue bow above the sofa.

As Nate rounded the corner of the sofa ahead of Becky to take a seat, he came to a dead halt.

"What?" Becky asked. She followed his horrified gaze and then took a quick step backward.

"That's my baby ChiChi," Mrs. McNally told them. "We had to leave her sister, Mimi, behind on Tulip Street, but ChiChi outlived her for quite a few years and, by the time she died, I was able to bring her here."

"Oh," Nate murmured politely, his face a little pale. "That's nice." Becky's mouth was too dry to comment. She had wanted to ask more about the dogs — especially Mimi — but was so shocked that she couldn't think of anything to say.

ChiChi had been preserved in a standing pose, her tail held out stiffly behind her and one paw raised as if she was about to step forward. Her eyes were made of glass. Becky shuddered.

Mrs. McNally settled them on the couch with glasses of water. Becky sipped at hers and tried determinedly not to look at ChiChi.

"So," Mrs. McNally said, looking at each of them with sharp blue eyes. "You're interested in the history of my house on Tulip Street."

"Uh, yeah," Nate said awkwardly, putting down his water glass. "Um, like we said, we're doing local history projects at school, and we're supposed to pick a local site to write about."

"Hmm." She nodded. "And what made you choose my house in particular?"

Becky and Nate exchanged a glance. The problem was that the McNally house was, except for all the rumors about supernatural horrors, pretty much just like all the other pleasant, deep-porched houses on their street.

"We live on Tulip Street," Becky said quickly, "and we always wondered about your house, because it's the only one that no one lives in."

Mrs. McNally's lips thinned slightly. "No one lives there because I own it, and I choose not to rent it out," she said. "However, the history of my family's house is similar to that of the other houses on the street. It was built in 1949, and the first owners were the Loomises, a serviceman who had been in World War Two and his wife and children." She paused and looked at them sternly over her glasses. "Shouldn't you two be taking notes?"

Becky felt her cheeks flush as she dug around in her backpack for a notebook and pencil. Nate, notebookless, looked at her helplessly, and she said, "I'll take notes, Nate. Um, you can take the lead with the interview."

"Okay," Nate said. "So, um, the Lewises were the first owners?"

"The Loomis family," Mrs. McNally said. "L-O-O-M-I-S."

Becky scribbled notes as Mrs. McNally filled them in on the history of the house. The problem was, it wasn't an especially interesting history. Mrs. McNally was right: There was nothing unusual about the history of the house, at least as she told it to them. Two families had lived there before the McNallys bought it when they were first married, and they had lived there until after Dr. McNally's death fifteen years before. That was when Mrs. McNally had moved to her apartment.

"So the house has just been sitting there empty for ten years?" Becky asked, interrupting Mrs. McNally.

"I have the house maintained," Mrs. McNally said, sitting up even straighter and frowning. "It's in quite good shape."

"But why don't you sell it or rent it out?" Becky asked tentatively. *Maybe she'll tell us the real reason: Because of the zombies!*

"Because I choose not to," Mrs. McNally said firmly.

"Um, there are a lot of stories about your old house," Nate said. "Like, that it's haunted or" — he glanced at Becky — "that zombies live there."

Mrs. McNally straightened even further and glared at them through her glasses, her eyes a bright, fierce blue. "That is completely absurd," she said. "I certainly hope your school isn't encouraging you to spread rumors about my property."

Nate stumbled over his words, apologizing and reassuring her that, no, the school didn't want him to write about that, and that of course they didn't believe the silly stories. Becky could just imagine the trouble they'd get into if Mrs. McNally complained and the school found out they'd been bothering her with a school assignment that didn't exist.

Once Mrs. McNally stopped looking quite so disapprovingly at them, Nate started asking her questions about the garden, and Becky was able to look around the room. She carefully avoided ChiChi's glazed dead stare while she pretended to take notes. A shadow box on the wall caught her eye. Inside it sat matching red and blue collars and red and blue dog tags, but only one red toy ball. She must have unintentionally made some kind of surprised sound, because Mrs. McNally stopped talking about her basil plants and gave Becky an inquisitive look.

"I was admiring the picture of your dogs up there," Becky said awkwardly. "They're so cute." The two Chihuahuas looked eager and happy in the picture in the shadow box, more lively than in the huge picture on the door, *much* more lively than ChiChi's poor stuffed body in the corner.

Smiling for the first time, Mrs. McNally rose and took the shadow box off the wall.

"Oh, yes," she said. "Mimi's in the blue collar here, and I'm sure you recognize ChiChi in the red one. Such good dogs." She sighed and handed Becky the shadow box.

"They're adorable," Becky told her, while her mind raced. "I have a dog, too." The little red ball covered with stars in the box looked so familiar. . . . Where had she seen something like it before?

The phone rang.

"Excuse me for a moment, children," Mrs. McNally said, and walked away.

Becky finally realized what she was looking at. "Look!" she hissed to Nate, and he looked. "This ball — Bear found a ball exactly like this, only blue, and really old and gross," she told him. "It must have been Mimi's ball that he dug up somewhere! Maybe *that's* why the zombie is mad at him."

"And check this out," Nate whispered back. He gestured at the bottom shelf of the bookcase. Becky saw several books about alternative medicine and some regular-looking medical books. But nestled by them on the end of the shelf were three books that seemed out of place: *Traversing the Boundaries Between the Living and the Dead*, *Herbal Powers*, and *Deadly Magicks*. "Write down these titles," Nate said. "We should try to find out stuff about them online."

Becky scribbled down the titles quickly. "Those books look like they definitely could have something to do with zombies," she said, keeping her voice too low for Mrs. McNally to hear.

Nate nodded in agreement. Glancing up and listening to hear if Mrs. McNally was still busy on the phone, he quickly slid *Traversing the Boundaries Between the Living and the Dead* out of the bookcase.

He searched through the index while Becky slid her notebook back into her bag and kept an ear out for Mrs. McNally.

"What are you looking for?" Becky asked.

"Something about objects," Nate said absently. "Since you realized Bear might have taken the zombie's ball. Okay. Found the chapter." He turned the pages, then read silently, biting his lip, and handed the book to Becky. "Here, look," he told her, tapping his finger on one particular spot.

The print in the book was old looking, thick, and black. Becky read:

Certain objects important to the walking dead in life can on occasion be buried with them and bring them peace; if these are removed from the dead's final resting place, they will walk again.

Chapter Twelve

That night, Becky dreamed about the McNally house again. She could hear the quick beat of her own heart thudding in her ears as she walked through its damp and musty rooms. She was sure she was looking for something, but she couldn't quite remember what.

And she had the disturbing feeling that something was following her. When she paused for a moment in the hall, she heard the *squelch* of small feet in the sodden fungus of the floor. Whipping around, Becky didn't see anything, but her heart began to thump even faster. She struggled to run. But the more she tried, the slower she went, her legs heavy. The floor sucked at her feet, and she found herself sinking ankle-deep in thick slime. Each time she pulled a foot out to take a step, the slime made a horrible slurping noise.

The light footsteps kept following her, squelching quickly along.

As she turned a corner, Becky found herself at a dead end and stopped. Turning, she found her way blocked by the Chihuahua. It looked at her balefully, its green eyes glowing, and began to move closer, teeth bared, body low, preparing to bite.

Becky woke up in the dark, sick and dizzy with fear, to the sound of thunder. She took deep breaths and thought about her and Nate's visit to Mrs. McNally to distract herself from her nightmare. After she'd made the connection about the dog toy, their meeting had been uneventful. Luckily, Mrs. McNally hadn't seen them looking at her books. They'd left her apartment on good terms soon after she came back into the room.

Before long, Becky drifted back to sleep.

The next day was a rain-filled Saturday. Becky spent her time inside searching the house, looking through drawers and cabinets, under her bed, in all the nooks and crannies of her room. The whole time, though, she knew it was pointless.

She remembered Bear bringing her a small blue star-spotted ball just before all the creepy stuff had started happening. That ball that was the counterpart of the red one in Mrs. McNally's shadow box — the ball that had woken up the zombie dog. She could picture it clearly, muddy and dingy and stinking with the same rotting smell that was everywhere now. And she remembered dropping it in the trash with disgust. The trash she had taken out to the curb the day she saw the zombie dog. She checked every spot she could think of where it might possibly be, just in case, but she was pretty sure the ball was gone for good.

"What are we going to do?" she asked Nate bleakly when he came over later in the afternoon. "The dog wants something that *I* threw away. We're never going to get rid of it."

Nate patted her on the back, wrinkling his nose a little at the rotting smell that still filled the house. "We'll figure it out," he said. "First, let's see if we can find out anything helpful about those books online."

They couldn't find anything about *Traversing the Boundaries Between the Living and the Dead,* and

Herbal Powers brought up too much stuff when they searched for it, none of it useful. But it turned out that some kind of witchy website quoted from *Deadly Magicks,* and it sounded like just what they needed.

"Look at this," Becky said excitedly. "*Deadly Magicks* actually talks about an herbal paste that it claims can 'put the undead to rest.' That would include zombies, right? It has some of the stuff we found online before: poppy seeds and cloves, but also white flour. You grind it together with pure water to make a paste. Oh . . . and an angel's trumpet flower. Wasn't that part on the voodoo website, too?"

Nate looked puzzled. "The first three things are easy enough, but what's an angel's trumpet flower?"

"Here," Becky said, finding a picture online. "Ooh, pretty. It says it's poisonous, though." The screen showed a photograph of a large shrub with oval leaves and dangling bell-like flowers.

"Huh." Nate looked closely at the picture. "Is it just me, or does that look kind of familiar?"

"Nah, they grow way down south," Becky said. "It says they're semitropical."

Nate frowned at the picture, and then his face lit up. "There's one of these next door," he announced. "I remember seeing it. It looked, like, more withered than the one in the picture, but I'm pretty sure it's the same thing."

"Are you sure?" Becky asked. It seemed suspiciously convenient.

"Don't you get it?" Nate said. He was starting to smile. "This almost proves that we're on the right track. The McNallys must have planted it because they needed the flowers so that they could raise the zombies and lay them to rest. It's the only explanation that makes sense."

Becky nodded. "Okay," she said. "So, if you're right, we can get everything we need to make the magic anti-zombie paste. But will that really put the zombie to rest even if we don't return its ball?"

"Well, we can at least try. Maybe we can find a similar ball and give it that, too," Nate said. "Let's go."

In the kitchen, Becky's dad was loading the dishwasher, standing right between Becky and the spice cupboard. Bear, who'd been lying under the kitchen table, came over and nosed Becky's hand, and she petted him. He looked thinner, she thought, and he hung by her side nervously instead of bouncing around.

"Hey, kids," her dad said, rinsing a plate. "Sure is raining out there today." There was a big pile of dishes in the sink, so it looked like he'd be there a while.

"Do we have cloves and poppy seeds and flour?" Becky asked him.

Her dad scratched his nose thoughtfully, dripping water onto his shirt from his wet hands. "I think we have cloves and flour, but probably not poppy seeds. Why?"

"Uh . . ." Becky thought hard for a second. "We thought maybe we'd make cookies later?" she said uncertainly.

"Okay," her dad said. "Sounds great, as long as you wash up your dishes. I'm sure you can find a recipe without poppy seeds. In fact, I don't think I've ever had cookies with poppy seeds in them."

He went on filling the dishwasher, then started scrubbing pots from the previous night's dinner, still blocking the spice cupboard.

"Want me to do that, Dad?" Becky offered at last.

Her dad seemed happy to hand off his dishrag. "Don't let Bear beg any human food," he warned, and headed off upstairs at last.

Becky took a little bowl and put cloves and flour in it, then grabbed a bottle of water from the fridge.

"What about poppy seeds?" Nate asked. "I don't think I've even ever seen them just for sale by themselves, have you?"

"No, but I think I know where to find some," Becky said, opening the bread box. She held up a poppy-seed bagel in triumph. "Ta-dah!"

"Good thinking," Nate said. He took the bagel and started scraping seeds into the bowl. "Don't forget the pots, though, or your dad will get mad."

"Ugh," Becky said, but went to work. When she finished and turned back around, Nate was handing a broken-off piece of bagel to Bear, who took it gratefully in his mouth, lay down, and started gnawing. "Hey!" she said. "My dad just said not to give him people food."

Nate blushed. "Sorry, I forgot," he said. "He really seemed to want it."

"I know," Becky told him. "He's such a good beggar that Jake and I are always feeding him from the table. So he just begs more."

"Should we brave the rain to go back to the McNallys' yard?" Nate asked her.

Becky left the water and bowl of flour and cloves on the counter, and she and Nate grabbed their rain jackets and headed hesitantly to the back door. "I guess there's no way to avoid it," she said nervously. Bear scrambled up to follow them, but Becky pushed him gently back as she opened the door. "Stay, Bear," she told him. Bear whined with disappointment as the door closed behind them.

As they pushed the loose board aside to cross into the McNallys', the steady rain seemed to increase. By the time they got through the opening, they were both very wet.

"Looks like the zombie dog's angry," Nate said, glancing up at the sky.

"Or not," Becky said, nervously peering around the yard. "Sometimes it just rains, right?"

Neither of them could keep from glancing over their shoulders, looking for shaking bushes or the zombie Chihuahua's tiny angry figure to suddenly appear. But everything stayed quiet.

They finally found the glossy-leafed bush that Nate had remembered. Becky's fingers fumbled at the wet petals of several of its orange flowers as she tried to pick them. It was so wet from the rain that the petals stuck to her hands and tore.

"Yuck," she said, tucking the battered flowers in her pocket. "Let's go."

Once they were back through the fence, they

both started to run. Mud splashed up from their sneakers and cold rain ran down the back of Becky's neck as, half laughing, they slammed the door of Becky's house behind them.

They left their shoes by the door, and Becky handed Nate a towel from the laundry basket.

"Let's get upstairs quick before your parents see us," Nate said. Bear came over and nosed at their cold hands and wet jeans and, as Becky petted him, she stooped down to pick up a toy he'd left by the door.

"This is perfect!" Becky exclaimed. The ball was not exactly like the Chihuahua's, but the right size, and blue with white dots that looked almost like stars.

Upstairs, Becky used pens and a ruler to mush the ingredients together while Nate checked the instructions on the Internet. They made sure to leave some aside in case they needed to try again. The wet flower petals tore into shreds, while the cloves and poppy seeds remained hard and whole, but the flour and water formed a sticky paste that held the other ingredients together.

"Becky," Nate said tensely, "it says here that the flowers can be really poisonous and not to get them in your eyes or mouth."

Becky stared at her hands for a minute and then got up and washed them for a long time with hot water and soap. "Thanks," she said. Before coming back, she slipped down to the kitchen and grabbed the big rubber cleaning gloves from under the sink. Back upstairs with the gloves on, she picked up the ruler again and poked at the mixture more gingerly.

When the ingredients seemed as combined as they were going to get, Becky and Nate scraped it up with pencils and glopped it onto Bear's ball. It was pretty gross and sticky when they finished, and Becky tucked the ball into a sandwich bag she'd brought upstairs with her.

"It's pretty dark out," Nate said, looking out the window. While they had been covering the ball with anti-zombie glop, the sun had set. "We'd better get going."

By unspoken agreement, they were both as quiet as possible creeping down the stairs, and Becky held her breath as she eased the front door open. The rain had lessened slightly, but it was still a steady drizzle. She could hear Bear's dog tags jingling in the kitchen; he was probably busy following her mother around in the hopes that she'd drop some food for him as she made dinner. Becky hoped he stayed occupied and didn't come out to find her. There would be no good way to explain this to her parents if they caught them now.

No one came, and she and Nate slipped out into the night. It was getting chillier in the evenings now, but Becky's shiver wasn't just from the cold. They'd agreed: It made sense to put the toy on the McNally property. But she felt really reluctant, scared to cross out of her own yard and back onto the zombie dog's territory again. She sort of wished Bear was with her, even though she knew that it was better to keep him away from danger.

In her own yard, the porch light illuminated the lawn a little bit but, once they slipped through the hole behind the loose board, everything was pitch-black. They stayed still, pressed close to one of the evergreen trees, waiting for their eyes to adjust to the darkness as water dripped down from the pine needles onto them. Gradually, the shapes became clearer around them. The bushes and the side of the house made darker patches in the night. The ground was muddy, and the slight sucking sound it made as they stepped reminded Becky uncomfortably of her dreams.

"The driveway," Nate whispered, his voice unsteady. Becky realized she was trembling, and she reached out for Nate without thinking about it. Ordinarily, she would have been too embarrassed to hold a boy's hand, but she needed something to hold on to. They gripped each other firmly as they headed toward the front of the McNally house. Becky's hands were freezing, but Nate's hand was comfortingly warm around hers. She was so grateful, suddenly, that she wasn't alone in this, and she squeezed Nate's hand.

They each stumbled a couple of times on their way, skidding on the wet grass, but they managed to keep each other from falling. The sickly rotting smell was stronger here than at Becky's house, and she shuddered as she imagined the smell rising from the peeling flesh of the little dog as perhaps it watched them unseen from the darker shadows around the house.

Finally, they saw the driveway, its concrete a paler patch ahead. Stepping onto it from the grass,

Becky hesitated and then shook the sticky blue ball out of its sandwich bag and dropped it into the middle of the driveway.

"What now?" she asked, hesitating, and Nate, still holding her hand, tugged her backward, off the driveway and back into the grass. Becky thought she felt something move beneath the sole of her shoe and flinched, hoping she wasn't stepping on one of those squirming insects she had seen in the daylight. A cold gust of wind shook the evergreens behind them noisily, and a few heavy drops of water landed on their backs. Becky shivered.

"We'll watch," Nate said. "Maybe we'll see if it accepts the ball or does anything with the paste."

They stood in silence, straining to see if anything was moving. Was there a darker shadow sliding across the pale concrete? Becky couldn't tell.

Suddenly, a branch snapped sharply behind them, and Becky and Nate both screamed.

Chapter Thirteen

As she screamed, Becky whipped around and saw a human shape behind her. *Not the dog*, she thought, and her scream cut off even as another part of her mind wondered, despairingly, if maybe Dr. McNally had created some human zombies, too. Maybe the whole house was crawling with them. Her heart was pounding hard in her chest, so hard that she could hear its beat.

"Hey," the shadowy figure said, coming forward. "Wow, what are you guys doing here?"

Paul, she realized, her heart calming, and she drew a deep breath.

"What are *we* doing here?" Nate said. "What are *you* doing here? You don't even live on this street! And it's raining out!" His normally laid-back voice was furious, and Becky could tell how scared he had been.

"I thought I'd check out the McNally house at night," Paul said. "It's only drizzling — I thought the rain would make an even cooler, spookier atmosphere. And I rode my bike over." Even though Becky couldn't really see his face, she thought he sounded embarrassed. He had something in his hands that reflected the little light there was, and Becky suddenly realized it was his camera. "I would have called you, but I didn't think you'd be into it. When we were over at Becky's house, you both seemed kind of irritated with the whole zombie thing."

Nate gave a surprised half laugh, but before either of them could answer, Paul was looking past them. "Hey," he said. "What's that?"

Becky whipped around, hearing Nate gasp behind her.

Something was moving slowly across the pale stretch of driveway toward where they had left the ball. Becky could hear nails clicking against the concrete. She peered forward through the darkness. Was the zombie sniffing at the ball and paste? It was so still for a moment, a huddled shape in just the right place. Maybe it would take the ball and go away, go back to rest again.

Slowly, the figure seemed to stiffen, and its head came up. Green eyes flashed eerily and the creature's thick wet growl filled the air. It charged past the ball, leaving it ignored — the paste untouched — and came toward them.

"Wow!" Paul said happily, raising his camera.

Nate and Becky each grabbed hold of one of Paul's arms and *ran*, slipping in the wet grass, shoving evergreen branches out of the way, fumbling at the fence between the houses to find the loose board, and finally racing across Becky's lawn toward her house. Her feet skidded on the grass and she almost fell, gripping Paul's arm to pull herself up.

The whole way, Becky was sure she heard tiny footsteps racing behind her, felt cold and clammy breath at her back. At every moment, she expected to feel small, sharp teeth on her leg.

Finally, they got inside the house. Becky slammed the door behind them and locked both locks. She thought she heard the scrape of claws against the door and another low snarl as it closed, but it was hard to tell over the patter of the rain shower.

Gasping, she looked around at the others, who were panting from the run and dripping water onto the floor. Nate was so pale that his freckles stood out clearly in little golden dots against his skin.

"That was amazing!" Paul said cheerfully. "Did you guys fix that up? What was it, like, some kind of motorized thing? Is it for Halloween?"

They both stared at him. Finally, Nate stretched what looked to Becky like a clearly false smile over his strained face. "Yeah," he said. "Yeah, we're working on it. It's not ready yet."

"So stay away from the McNally house, okay?" Becky added, her voice squeaky with nervousness. "Because it's not ready."

"Becky?" her dad called, coming down the stairs. He frowned when he saw Paul. "I didn't realize you had another friend over. It's almost dinnertime."

"I know, Dad," Becky said quickly. "Paul just came by to get Nate. They're going now." Nate and Paul, thankfully, nodded.

Her dad waited. After a moment, it was clear that he was waiting for the boys to leave. Becky hesitated. What if the zombie dog was out there? She was almost sure she had heard claws against the door.

But her dad was waiting. She and Nate stared at each other, frozen.

Finally, Paul reached out and unlocked the door before Becky could warn him. "See you later, Becky," he said, swinging it open. "Bye, Mr. Nolan."

A cold breeze swept in the door, bringing the sound of rustling leaves. There was nothing waiting on the porch. Nate followed Paul out, grimacing back at Becky. At least they were heading *away* from the McNally house, toward Nate's end of the street.

Becky had dinner with her family, barely able to concentrate on what she was eating or to follow what her parents and Jake were talking about. She kept thinking of the zombie Chihuahua's angry snarl and how it had charged toward them after sniffing the ball.

It must not have fallen for their trick, Becky thought, because that certainly hadn't been anything like being put to rest. It was more like the zombie was angry they'd tried to fool it. Clearly the paste wasn't going to work without the right ball.

She went up to her room, thinking hard about what they could do to stop the zombie. Later, once everyone had gone to sleep, she tiptoed down to sneak Bear upstairs. Poor Bear had been so nervous and agitated lately that she couldn't stand to leave him alone downstairs. He stuck close to her, his fur brushing against her leg, while they were going upstairs, and then slunk under her bed when they got into her room.

Becky climbed back into bed and lay down, listening to Bear's little whines slowly change to steady breathing. Her stomach hurt with anxiety, and she crossed her arms over it, clutching her elbows.

She only had one idea, and she hated it. She wasn't the kind of person who stole and lied, but the only way she could see that they might get rid of the zombie was if they stole the ball — the *other* ball, the one that had belonged to ChiChi, Mimi's sister — from Mrs. McNally's shadow box.

Chapter Fourteen

The next day was Sunday, and Becky was putting the finishing touches on her anti-zombie plan when the phone rang.

Becky was happily surprised to hear the voice on the other end say, "Hey, it's Tonya."

They chatted for a little while, and Becky was glad to be distracted from all things zombie. Then Tonya said, "Paul e-mailed me the pictures he took at the house next door to you last night."

"Yeah?" Becky said uneasily. She remembered how freaked out Tonya had seemed the afternoon they had all heard the weird howling from next door. The last thing she wanted was to encourage the freaky rumors about her street, or worse, for anyone to find out there actually *was* a zombie.

"It was cool," Tonya said, laughing a little bit. "What did you use, some kind of old stuffed animal? And maybe Christmas lights? I couldn't see that well in the picture, but it looked really interesting. And Paul said it moved, too. How'd you do that?"

"Um, a remote control thing," Becky said, thinking fast.

"Are you going to use it for Halloween?" Tonya asked.

"Maybe," Becky said cautiously. "We haven't figured it out completely, though. It might not work."

"Awesome," Tonya said. "I wanted to say" — she hesitated — "um, that I was sorry I got so freaked out just from a dog howling when I was over there. I think it's really creative and cool the way you and Nate are using the rumors about your street to make scary, fun stuff."

"Um." Becky was so surprised by this that she couldn't quite think what to say. "Uh, thanks."

"Anyway," Tonya went on. "I was mostly calling because I wanted to ask you about the art club. You're in it, right?"

"Oh, yeah!"

"Well, I was thinking about joining. I mean, I'm not good at drawing like you are," Tonya said, sounding embarrassed, "but I like making stuff, and I thought it might be fun. It's on Wednesdays, right?"

"You should join," Becky said. "It's really fun."

"Yeah?" Tonya asked. "It's just . . . I don't really know anyone in it except for you, and I was worried they might all be really good artists and that I would be sort of the lame one in the group."

"Not at all," Becky said, laughing. "I didn't really know anyone either, but everyone seems nice, and they're just normal people. Like, it's not van Gogh in there, just people who like doing art projects."

They talked for a while longer, and Becky got off the phone feeling good for the first time in a while. It was nice to know that Tonya didn't *really* believe there was something evil about her street (even if she was wrong), and fun to think about spending more time with Tonya and working on projects with her in art club. Maybe they could actually go ahead and *do* something spooky for Halloween based on the rumors about the McNally house. If she and Nate managed to get rid of the zombie first.

Becky had to spend the rest of the morning at Jake's soccer game, even though it was still gray and raining on and off. She worried the whole time about what might be going on back at the house, but finally, in the afternoon, she and Nate took the bus over to Vantage Place once more.

"Are you sure this is a good idea?" Nate asked as they walked inside the building. He swallowed unhappily. "Are we — are we really just going to *take* it?"

"I know," Becky said, and heard the guilty quaver in her own voice. She spoke in a whisper and smiled shakily at the security guard, who seemed to be looking at them suspiciously. "But I don't see what else we can do. We have to try this." Her stomach was hurting, and she already felt horrible.

It would be *wrong* to steal ChiChi's ball from Mrs. McNally, she knew. Mrs. McNally was clearly devoted to — or more like obsessed with — her dogs. Becky shuddered at the thought of seeing the preserved ChiChi again.

Becky had taken another of Bear's balls — a red one this time — to replace ChiChi's ball in the shadow box, but she didn't think Mrs. McNally would be deceived at all. But what else could she do? *Getting rid of the zombie is more important than Mrs. McNally's feelings*, she told herself. But she didn't like it.

The night before, for a moment, she had really believed the other ball was going to work. The zombie Chihuahua had seemed to give it a lot of attention, its hunched form crouching over it for a long time in the darkness before it had snarled and turned its glowing gaze on them. If they could just get a ball the dog would accept, Becky was sure (well, almost sure) that their plan would work. She didn't want to think about the alternative.

When they reached Mrs. McNally's condo, Becky muttered, "Here goes nothing," and tapped at the door.

Mrs. McNally did not look especially pleased to see them. "You're back," she said, raising her eyebrows a little. "Was there something else you wanted to ask me, children? You'll forgive me if we keep this short, but I have my book group in half an hour." She didn't move away from the door, and Becky looked desperately at Nate, who went into his prepared speech.

"I'm sorry to bother you again, Mrs. McNally," he said, blue eyes wide, "but I told my mom about how you had ChiChi . . . um . . . preserved, and she, um, really wanted to know who did it for you. Because she has this cat who's pretty old, and, uh . . ."

He sounded really nervous and unsure, and part of Becky expected Mrs. McNally to know he was lying.

But instead the older lady opened her door wider. "Come in," she said to them. "I think I can get what you need for your mother."

Inside, she led Nate down the hall to look through her filing cabinet for the information. Becky lingered in the living room, waiting until they were around the corner and out of view, then pulled out Bear's ball. She flinched as she caught the glassy eyes of ChiChi, poised beside the couch, and hesitated. She almost wanted to apologize to the dog. But Becky turned away and reached up to take the shadow box down from the wall. Mimi and ChiChi were staring at her from their photograph, their brown eyes wide and appealing. She pulled her hand back, a wave of guilt washing over her.

I can't do this, she realized, putting Bear's ball back in her pocket. *I can't steal ChiChi's ball.*

She had a new plan of action, and she didn't know if it would work, but it seemed like the only choice left.

*   *   *

Nate and Mrs. McNally came back down the hall a few minutes later, Nate holding a manila folder that must have been full of taxidermist information. Becky stood up and took a deep breath.

"Mrs. McNally," she said, "I'm sorry, but we didn't tell you the truth about why we came to see you today."

Mrs. McNally turned to Nate inquiringly and raised one eyebrow, her face chilly. Nate turned beet red but nodded, shamefaced.

"We were hoping to talk to you about Mimi," Becky went on, "and about your house." She could see that Mrs. McNally was about to say no: Her face was drawing into a frown, her lips turning down. "*Please*, Mrs. McNally," she said. "Everything's gone really wrong, and I think you're the only one who can help us."

Becky could hear the desperation in her own voice. Something about what she said or how she said it must have gotten through to Mrs. McNally, because she stopped looking annoyed and started looking worried.

"You'd better tell me all about it from the beginning," Mrs. McNally said finally, and sat down.

They told Mrs. McNally everything. Becky did most of the talking, Nate sitting beside her and chiming in occasionally with details she had forgotten, but mostly just offering moral support, his eyes steady and reassuring.

Mrs. McNally listened. A couple of times she frowned and drew breath as if she was going to start arguing with them, but she didn't say anything.

At last, Becky said, "So . . . Bear's toy didn't work. But we thought that if we tried ChiChi's toy, maybe that would work better. Since it's like Mimi's, except a different color, and it belonged to Mimi's sister, so she would be familiar with it." Becky took a breath. "Mimi — she's — it's not safe. She could bite other animals, or people even, and turn them into zombies. She's angry — she snapped at me — and she might bite someone eventually. And . . . it's not right, her being like that. That's not how a dog is supposed to be." Becky hadn't thought about it before, but now she did, contrasting her happy, lively Bear with the green-eyed, snarling creature that dragged itself through the darkness. *Poor Mimi*, she thought. *I'm sure she never wanted this.*

Becky's voice trailed off into silence, and Mrs. McNally didn't answer immediately. She was staring past them at the shadow box on the wall. Slowly, she rose and took down the shadow box.

"Mimi was a good dog," she said finally, tracing her fingers above the little dog's picture. "My husband and I loved her, her and ChiChi both, and they were so sweet together. ChiChi was heartbroken when Mimi died. And then," her voice went hoarse, "Mimi became my husband's first successful experiment. We were horrified at what she became, and we managed to put her back to rest."

"How?" Nate asked quickly. "How did you make her go to sleep?"

"With the voodoo paste you two found the recipe for. That's why we had the angel's trumpet bush: We researched to find out what the mythology said would be effective. That recipe is the only nonviolent solution I know of. We couldn't bear to have Mimi suffer. But in this instance, she woke up because her ball was taken, so the paste won't work by itself. If Mimi's ball is gone, ChiChi's *might* work. But I can't promise it will." Mrs. McNally sighed, and reached over to stroke stuffed ChiChi next to the couch. Becky flinched a little as Mrs. McNally touched ChiChi, but could see the sadness in the woman's face.

"Mimi loved her sister," Mrs. McNally said softly. "And we loved them both. That's the reason I haven't been able to make myself put the house on the market. I couldn't disturb Mimi's last resting place, and I couldn't make myself face the evidence of what happened in that house." She stared down at the picture in the shadow box for a moment more, pressing her fingers against the glass so hard that their tips were white with pressure. "Yes, I will help you," she said at last. "Mimi needs this."

She opened the shadow box and slowly took out the red star-spotted ball and held it for a moment before handing it to Becky. "Good luck," she said. "I hope it gives Mimi her rest."

Becky felt like she was going to cry. "We'll do our best," she told Mrs. McNally, squeezing the ball tightly. "We'll try to take care of Mimi."

Chapter Fifteen

There was nothing to do now except wait for it to get dark so they could try again. It was raining again, and heavier than before, but they agreed they still wanted to do it that night.

They were in the kitchen, nervously passing the time with Jake.

"Touchdown!" Becky shouted as she flicked the triangle of paper between the goalposts of her little brother's fingers. Next to her, Nate was busily folding his own triangle.

"Ten to seven, sucker," she said to him. "Your turn." Nate was just opening his mouth to reply when her mom came in.

"Nate's mom is on the phone," she said, and Nate got up and took the call in the hall. "So," she said to

Becky when Nate was out of the room, "Nate's been over a lot lately."

Becky had a quick flash of fear — did her mom know what they were up to? Then she looked at her mom's expectant half smile and got it: Her mom thought she and Nate were *dating*. "Jeez, Mom," she said defensively. "We're friends, okay?"

They *were* just friends, right? She thought about how cute Nate was, and how nice, and felt her cheeks burning.

Her mom just shrugged and looked irritatingly smug.

When Nate came back in, he was biting his lip, worried. "My mom says I have to come home," he said.

"Can we meet when it gets dark?" Becky whispered. She glanced at Jake, who was busy unfolding one of the paper footballs and seemingly not paying any attention to them. Her mom was looking in the refrigerator, and Becky hoped she couldn't hear from where she was standing. "To ... take care of the other thing."

Nate grimaced apologetically. "Once I get home, I don't think I can get out again," he whispered back.

"I've got homework, and my parents are super alert. I'm pretty sure they'd catch me if I tried to sneak out. I don't think you should do it alone, though," he went on, frowning. "It's not safe. Maybe later this week?"

"Maybe," Becky said. She was feeling resolved, though. Mimi was a danger to the whole neighborhood. Now that they had something that might work, might put her to rest, Becky knew that she had to try it right away. Her heart was hammering just at the idea of going alone, but she knew she would be anxious until it was over. She forced a smile onto her face. If Nate couldn't come, there was no reason to make him worry about it all night. She'd be okay. Probably.

After she saw him off, Becky grabbed the rubber gloves from the kitchen again and went up to her room. She found the baggie of dry ingredients that they had thankfully set aside before, and she went through the same procedure they had done the previous night: mushing the flower petals together with the cloves, poppy seeds, white flour, and bottled water. She painstakingly painted it onto ChiChi's ball with the eraser of her pencil, careful not to spill any of the poisonous glop.

It was all so familiar, but it felt weird without Nate beside her. Becky wished she wasn't doing it alone — she wasn't completely sure she could handle it.

Everything was ready even before dark, and Becky waited through dinner, listening to the rain pounding at the windows, and picking at her food. Her parents were downstairs and she couldn't sneak out — they would want to know where she was going in the middle of such a dreary night. So she brushed Bear's fur and watched TV with her mother without really seeing what was on the screen, counting down the minutes until she could say she was going to bed.

Finally, she said good night. Once she was upstairs, though, Becky sat on the edge of her bed in the dark and listened, jiggling her leg anxiously, waiting for her parents to go to bed. She looked out the window occasionally, half expecting to see a hunched shadow lurching painfully across the grass, eerie green eyes flashing up at her. But zombie Mimi didn't appear. Becky closed her eyes and breathed deeply, telling herself, *It will be all right.*

Once Becky thought that her parents must be asleep, she tiptoed down the stairs, tightly clutching the sandwich bag with ChiChi's ball in it. As she stepped into the hall, a floorboard creaked loudly and Becky froze, waiting for someone to call down and ask what she was doing. But there was no noise from upstairs. No one had heard.

There *was* a noise from the kitchen, though. Apparently Bear had heard her just fine. His tags jingled and he gave a short, eager huffing noise from inside his crate. She could hear him climbing to his feet, delighted that Becky had come down to see him. She went to the crate and petted him through the bars as his tail thrashed happily back and forth.

"Good boy," she whispered. "Shush, now. Shush."

Bear quieted, but as soon as she moved away from his crate, he gave a low bark, watching her attentively. *Come back*, he was obviously saying. *Surely you're not leaving so soon?*

"Shh, Bear," Becky whispered. "It's okay." She moved toward the back door and gingerly put on her raincoat. Bear tensed. "Shh," she said again, holding her hands up to him in a *stay*. She laid her hand on the doorknob and Bear barked sharply, louder this time.

He didn't want her to go. Becky knew Bear, and she was a hundred percent sure that, if she walked out the back door right then, he was going to howl and bark until her parents were up and looking for her, and then he wasn't going to calm down until he had Becky back. Bear loved her, and he was stubborn, and he did not want her to go outside alone right then.

"Oh, Bear," she whispered, feeling close to tears. "I have to." He went quiet and looked at her, his tail held low and wagging uncertainly. When she reached for the doorknob again, he barked again, once, louder still, his eyes on her.

"Dumb dog," Becky whispered fiercely, feeling intensely grateful. She walked over to Bear's crate and crouched down close to him. "Do you want to come with me? Is that what you want?" she asked. "Wouldn't you rather stay safe, Bear?"

Bear met her eyes, waiting, and Becky opened his crate. He came out and licked her quickly on the cheek, but still seemed anxious. He went past her, stopping to wait for her by the back door.

"Oh, good dog," she whispered fervently, realizing how glad she was not to have to go alone.

One hand on Bear's collar and one hand laid protectively over the lump of ChiChi's ball in her jacket pocket, Becky led Bear down the porch steps and across the lawn. The wind had picked up, and she blinked away the rain blowing into her face. As they approached the loose board in the fence, Bear began to slow, tugging against Becky's grasp on his collar. Just like the last time she had taken this journey, thunder boomed overhead. This was turning into a real storm. Bear growled low in his throat.

"I'm sorry, boy, but we have to," Becky said softly.

To her surprise, Bear stopped tugging away from her and nosed forward.

"Good boy," she said, and pushed the loose board aside. She and Bear wriggled through, gave their eyes a moment to adjust to the darkness, and headed around the side of the McNally house. Bushes rustled beside them, and Becky sucked in her breath. *It's just the wind*, she told herself, *and the rain on the branches.* But she didn't really believe it.

They reached the driveway without seeing anything, and Becky quickly laid the ball down in the center of the drive and backed carefully away. The rain was even harder now, and Becky's hair was getting plastered across her forehead and shoulders. Raindrops ran into her eyes and mouth.

"Mimi!" she called, the name feeling strange in her mouth. She peered toward the dark shape that was the house in front of her. She tried to speak loudly over the wind and rain. "This is ChiChi's ball. I'm sorry, we don't have yours anymore. But it's your sister's, and your owner sent it with us. Please, I hope it's enough for you."

From behind her came a wet, throbbing snarl.

Becky whipped around just as lightning flashed. The dog was right behind her. It was right *there*, closer than she'd ever been to it. Its teeth were bared in a growl, and its eyes were glowing savagely at her. She could see the skin curling back dryly from its hanging ear. Becky backed away, a whimper catching in her throat.

Zombie Mimi looked angry. She wasn't even looking at the ball. The horrible smell, which Becky had gotten so used to over the past couple of days that she hadn't even really noticed it tonight, washed over her, and she almost gagged.

"No," Becky whispered. She was shaking so hard that everything around her seemed to be moving gently. Her eyes met the zombie's, and she saw how angry and confused it was, saw its eyes shift to her neck and imagined it leaping for her throat. *I don't want to be a zombie*, she thought desperately. Her mind raced, trying to figure out what would be the best exit strategy.

Then Bear barked, one loud, commanding bark.

The zombie dog's eyes shifted to him, and she growled again. Bear, businesslike, turned around and walked to the ball behind him, dropped his head, and nosed it carefully toward the other dog. Becky wanted to grab Bear and pull him away, but she couldn't make herself move.

The zombie Chihuahua — *Mimi*, Becky thought — stopped growling and watched Bear, her head cocked to one side, her eyes flashing green. Bear barked again, once. After a moment, the zombie dog whined, a questioning whine with an unnatural little waver in it, as if it was being pulled from a throat that didn't quite work right anymore. Then she came forward less aggressively, limping slowly. Her tail was drooping, and she ducked her head as she got closer to Bear, looking smaller and less fearsome. Becky felt a sudden stab of sympathy for her: She seemed so lonely.

Bear backed away as Mimi came toward him, his tail held high over his back, his eyes fixed on her. Mimi lowered her head to the ball, nudged it, and carefully picked it up. Her ragged tail wagged once, slowly. Then, without looking at them again, Mimi walked toward the house, disappearing into the darkness, her sister ChiChi's ball in her mouth. Bear stood still and watched her go, and then turned toward Becky, his tail wagging.

The rain stopped as suddenly as if someone had turned off a faucet. Becky, dripping, looked up to see a clear sky full of stars.

"Oh, Bear," she whispered. Her heart was pounding. Somehow, though, she didn't think they were in danger now. She wiped Bear's nose carefully with a wet leaf, to get all of the poisonous paste off. "Come on," she said, and Bear went with her back around the house and through the hole in the fence to her own yard.

Once they were inside the house, she couldn't stop petting Bear, sinking her hands into his thick damp fur and laying her face against his head. She felt like crying out of sheer relief. It was over. Wasn't it? Mimi had taken the ball. The rain had stopped. The smell was dissipating. She got Bear a treat from his special treat jar. He wasn't supposed to get them all the time, but he definitely deserved one tonight.

Was it over? Was Mimi at rest now? Becky thought so, but how could she know?

At last, Bear sleepily got up, licked her on the cheek, and walked calmly to his crate. He shifted around on his pillow, making himself comfortable, and then settled down, rested his head on his paws, and gave a blissful sigh. Becky smiled. He'd been so agitated, and now he was fine. He knew, she was sure, that Mimi was at rest again.

Her cell phone was on the counter and she picked it up to text Nate. He was probably asleep, but he would get the message in the morning.

Mimi's gone, she texted. Bear saved me.

Chapter Sixteen

Becky called Mrs. McNally the next morning before school, from her room. She thought Mrs. McNally deserved to know as soon as possible that her beloved Mimi was at rest again.

"She took the ball," she told her, "and went back inside. The rain stopped. Mimi looked . . . happier."

There was a little pause before Mrs. McNally answered her. "Thank you, Becky," the older lady said quietly. "We . . . my husband and I made a mistake when we tried to bring Mimi back. It was painful to think that she was a zombie again, and I am glad you were able to give her peace."

When Becky pressed the END button on her phone, there were tears in her eyes. Not sad tears, but sympathetic ones. She loved Bear so much and she could imagine wanting to bring him back no matter what — but she could also imagine the pain of realizing that bringing him back had led to his suffering. Now that Mimi was at rest, Mrs. McNally could feel happier, too.

"I still can't believe you went without me," Nate said as they headed through the halls at the end of the school day. "What if something had happened?"

Becky smiled. "Bear was looking out for me," she said. "And, you know, I think his behavior's already getting better. Without Mimi around to scare him, I'm sure he'll be the perfect dog."

Nate raised an eyebrow at her, and she shrugged. "I had a good idea, though. I suggested to my parents that I could take Bear to obedience classes at the community center. He could probably stand some better training. And the idea made my dad feel a lot better about keeping him."

They were almost to the doors when she saw Charlotte ahead of them and hurried to catch up with her. It had been a while since she'd thought about Charlotte — the zombie trouble had taken up all of her energy.

"Hey, Charlotte," she said impulsively. "Can I talk to you for a second?"

Charlotte stopped and turned, and gave her a tentative smile. "Of course you can," she said softly.

Becky glanced out the doors. They had a few minutes before the buses would leave, and she was supposed to meet Tonya first. They'd decided to try to make their own tempera paints for art club tomorrow. But Tonya wasn't outside yet: She had a moment.

"Are we still friends, Charlotte?" she asked. "We haven't hung out lately, and I know you've made new friends in chorus. I'm sorry I got mad at you for thinking my neighborhood was creepy."

"I'm sorry, too," Charlotte said in a rush. "I definitely still want to be friends. I should have been on your side when you were upset about the stories everyone was telling. It wasn't nice for me to say what I did." She was fiddling nervously with her watchband, and looked sad.

"It's okay," Becky said. "But the stories about the McNally house really aren't true. There's nothing scary there." She was pretty sure she could say that now: Mimi the zombie dog was definitely gone, Bear's behavior had indicated that, and the smell that had hung over the neighborhood had been gone when she woke up that morning. For the first time in days, Becky had been able to breathe clean fresh air, and that had felt wonderful.

And Becky was also pretty sure that the other rumors — the witch covens and vampires and were-wolves — had never been true.

Charlotte bit her lip. "I know," she said slowly. "I haven't known how to talk to you about it, but I really wanted to apologize. I also was kind of using that as an excuse for not hanging out as much. I wanted to do more stuff with Lila and the kids from chorus, and I didn't know how to tell you." Becky's heart sank a little — Charlotte had pretended to be scared of Becky's neighborhood just so she didn't have to feel guilty about ditching Becky to hang out with her friends from chorus? That was weird, and not something a good friend should do.

Charlotte rushed into her speech again. "I'm still your friend, Becky," she said. "I'll always be your friend, if you want me. It's just that last year we spent all our time with just each other, and I guess" — she ducked her head and looked up at Becky nervously — "I handled making other friends really badly. But I don't want to *not* be friends with you. I really don't."

Becky looked out the windows toward the buses and saw Tonya standing with Nate and Paul and Nate's other friend Noah. They were all laughing about something, and she realized that if Charlotte hadn't turned away from her for a while, she never would have had Nate for a study partner or invited Tonya over to her house — she would have been just doing stuff with Charlotte. Becky might never have had the possibilities of these other new friends, people who she might like even better than Charlotte.

"I think you were right, Charlotte," she said. "We should hang out with other people."

Charlotte's face fell for a moment, and Becky reached out and hugged her quickly. After all, Charlotte was the first friend she'd made here, and even if they were both changing, she still *liked* her. "But we can still be friends, too," she reassured her. "It doesn't have to be one or the other."

Charlotte smiled. "I'm glad," she said. "Do you want to go to the movies with me and Lila this weekend?"

"Maybe," Becky said. "Call me and let me know when." They pushed out through the doors into the afternoon sunshine together and then headed in different directions. Becky caught up with Tonya and Nate and the other guys just before they got on the bus, and they all sat together.

Paul had his pictures of the zombie dog, and Becky grabbed them. In the photographs, she could barely see the outline of Mimi's body against the shadows, but her eyes glowed eerily, glaring out of the darkness.

"I can't wait to see what it's going to look like by Halloween," Paul said eagerly, and Nate and Becky exchanged a glance.

"I don't know if that's going to happen," Becky said slowly.

"Yeah," Nate said. "We ran into a little snag with the design."

"Oh, too bad," Tonya said. "Maybe we can make something else, though. They have this cool glow-in-the-dark paint at the art store near the mall."

As they came up the street from the bus stop, they were making plans for different Halloween decorations and costumes. Becky invited everyone over to come up with designs. Noah, it turned out, thought he could fiddle with the engine from a remote-control car to make a ghost swoop forward when trick-or-treaters came toward the front steps.

"We should definitely do it at your house, Becky," Noah said. "Because everyone's already freaked out by all the ghost stories people tell about the house next door to you."

It doesn't matter, Becky realized. Now that she'd faced the real zombie dog and laid it to rest, all the other stories people told about the McNally house just seemed silly, the way Nate had always thought. It would be fun to give the trick-or-treaters a harmless little thrill.

"Maybe we could make, like, a cauldron of witch's brew and have dry ice or something making steam," she said. "We should decorate the whole house so it's really scary."

Everyone started talking at once, shooting out suggestions, but Becky didn't really hear them. She had noticed what was happening on her lawn.

Bear was standing on the grass, his head lowered and his tail wagging uncertainly. At the corner of the fence, the loose board shook hard and then, slowly, deliberately, pushed away from the rest of the fence, leaving an opening.

Becky froze. Was there another zombie animal? Something was coming through the fence, something pale and furry. *It can't be the Chihuahua!* she thought. *It just can't. It's over.*

A small, ragged kitten popped through the hole and out into the yard. Becky breathed a little easier for a second, and then she thought: Hadn't Dr. McNally done other experiments? What if other zombies were waking up?

If the kitten attacked Bear now, there would be no way to stop it. Becky was too far away.

She watched as Bear lowered his head, nosing unsurely at the kitten, who reared back a little. *Oh, Bear*, she thought. Why didn't he run away?

The kitten bunched its legs beneath itself and leaped into the air, landing on Bear's back. Then it turned in a circle, its little paws kneading at the loose skin on the back of Bear's neck. Bear held still, then turned his head, trying to see along his own back, and accidentally turned himself all the way around, a baffled expression on his face.

The kitten lay down and curled itself into a ball, secure on Bear's broad back. *Not a zombie*, Becky realized with relief. *Just a kitten*. Finally, Bear gave up on seeing his own back and flopped down on the ground with a great doggy sigh. He closed his eyes and, by the time they reached Becky's house, he and the kitten both seemed to have fallen asleep.

"Is he going to take off if we go inside and leave him asleep out front?" Nate asked. "You know your parents will freak out if he's wandering the neighborhood again."

Becky shrugged. "I think one good thing about everything that's happened is that Bear will stick closer to home from now on," she said. "But we'll sit out on the porch until he wakes up."

She ran into the house to get snacks and drinks for everyone, and the five of them stretched out across the swing and benches on the porch, everyone suggesting crazy Halloween decorations and costumes. Bear whuffed peacefully in his sleep and, after a while, the kitten rolled off his back and curled up next to his side instead. Jake and the Kolodny kids — who turned out to be the owners of the new kitten, who'd been out roaming the neighborhood — showed up a few minutes later and hung out with the older kids, stealing cookies and suggesting completely impractical Halloween ideas. Jake added werewolf to his costume list.

"You can't be a ninja vampire cat soccer player *werewolf*," Becky told him. "Cat and werewolf cancel each other out. Maybe just a vampire ninja soccer player werewolf, and leave off the cat?"

Jake frowned and shook his head, and Nate laughed, pushing his shaggy hair out of his eyes with the back of his hand. "How about a ninja vampire soccer player were*cat*?" he asked, and Jake looked pleased.

On the other side of the fence, Becky could see the boarded-over windows of the McNally house, but they didn't remind her of eyes anymore. No one was watching her from the empty house now. There wasn't anything scary over there anymore. She bit into a cookie.

The zombie dog was gone. Bear was going to be allowed to stay. She'd made a couple of really good friends. And Becky's new house felt like home again.

HERE'S A BONE-CHILLING
SNEAK PEEK AT ANOTHER
ROTTEN APPLE BOOK!

MEAN GHOULS

The ride to Zombie Academy was the longest two hours of Megan's life.

When she arrived at the front gate, the first thing she saw was a very cute boy her own age. He had dark skin, thick brown hair, and wore jeans with a white T-shirt and a sweater vest. The glassy look in his eyes might have been a symptom of zombitus, or it might have been that the boy just played a lot of video games. It was impossible for Megan to tell the difference.

For a moment Megan wondered if she was at the right school.

"Hi. I'm Sam," the boy greeted her.

"Hi." Megan went to shake his hand but as she touched him, his thumb fell off. It wasn't bloody or gross. It simply dropped to the dirt like a loose button or a bit of lint.

"Oh, uh . . ." She grimaced, glancing between his four-fingered hand and the thumb. She had no clue what she should do. "I'm sorry," Megan said at last.

"No problem." Sam quickly picked his thumb up and blew off the dust. "I lose parts all the time. The nurse sews them back on for me. We've tried every kind of thread. Nothing holds very well." He pulled a small Ziploc baggie out of his pocket and showed Megan his pinky toe. "Might as well get two digits done at the same time." He put his thumb in the bag and then stuffed it into his pocket.

Sam thanked the limo driver. Megan hadn't looked at the man before; she'd only seen the back of his head while he drove. And now she was glad she hadn't looked. His head was barely attached to his neck. It kept lolling over to one side or the other. One of his eyes was hanging loosely from some kind of oozing stringy stuff. And though she hadn't noticed it from the backseat, *whew*, the guy stunk!

It was impossible to imagine how he'd driven the car safely. If her parents had seen him, they'd never have let Megan in the limo. No wonder he'd kept the tinted windows rolled up and shouted, "Get in!" to Megan. She was glad to have arrived safely and relieved when the limo drove off, leaving her on the sidewalk with Sam.

While Sam got her suitcase, Megan grabbed her backpack. It was then that Megan finally took a good look around.

Zombie Academy was straight out of one of Zach's horror movies: a castle nestled among the trees, with a high fence and a huge iron gate surrounding the complex. Megan wondered if the gate kept healthy people out or the zombie kids in. She didn't really want to know the answer.

The castle itself was made of stone. It was pretty, but also a place you'd expect to be haunted. Or infested by the living dead. There was a tower on each side of the gate, and small slit windows. Megan thought she saw some girls peeking out of one of the windows, but when she squinted for a better look, they were gone.

"Come on," Sam told Megan. "The outside of the school is kind of spooky, but the inside has been totally redone. A long time ago this millionaire, Lewis Jones, got the zombitus virus and decided to spend all his money looking for a cure. When other people got infected, he invited them to come to his estate. Then, he went around the world to find known zombies and invited them to come here, too. Mr. Jones pays for everything." Sam added, "Of course, once the researchers find the antidote, the deal is he gets the first shot."

"What about the other Zombie Academies?" Megan asked.

"Yep, he built those, too," Sam said. "You'll meet Mr. Jones later. He's like a grandfather to everyone who lives here."

Sam let Megan in through the gate, then locked it behind her.

She gave him a puzzled look.

"I've been here a long time," he explained. "I like to help out. When I heard you were coming, I offered to come meet you. There's no one who knows their way around this place better than me. Except Mr. Jones, of course." Sam led her into the main part of the castle. "So, Megan Murry, welcome to Zombie Academy."

"Whoa." Megan was amazed. The interior of the building really didn't match the outside. The halls were filled with beautiful museum-quality paintings and sculptures, modern lighting, leafy tropical plants, and, in the middle of the entry, a glass elevator that led to the higher floors. It reminded Megan of a hotel her family had stayed at on a vacation to Hawaii once. There was even a small waterfall flowing into a koi pond.

"Come on." Sam set his four-fingered hand on Megan's back and led her into the elevator. "Level five is the dormitory. I'll show you your room. Then you need to check in at the nurse's office. She'll give you your class schedule." He patted his pocket. "We can go together."

"The girls in the dorm room next to yours are mean. Really mean." Sam grimaced as they walked by a purple-painted door decorated with three cutout gold stars. Each star had a name on it: Brooke. Betsy. Brenda.

"'Zom-Bs,'" Megan read the big letters printed above the names.

"My advice," Sam said, "is to ignore them. Fly under their radar. The Bs are nasty."

Megan thought about Brett's sister, Hailey Hansen, and her gang of mean girls. "Gotcha," Megan told Sam. "I know girls like that at home."

"We all do," Sam said with a sigh.

He knocked on a plain brown wooden door. "Home, sweet home."

The girl who answered the door wore a black dress with black shoes and tights. Her hair was dyed black. Her eyeliner was black and so was her eye shadow. Even her lipstick was black. She looked like a vampire, not like someone with zombitus.

"Hey-ya, Happy," Sam said as if the girl's appearance was totally normal. "Do any painting today?"

Happy didn't seem very happy. She sulked across the room and turned an easel to show Sam a fresh canvas.

"Finished it," she said in a voice that sounded like Eeyore from *Winnie the Pooh*.

The painting was, well, black. Completely black to the edges of the canvas.

"Wow!" Sam exclaimed. "That's one of your best!"

Happy moaned. "It's not very good."

Sam turned to Megan. "Picasso had his blue stage. Happy's in a darker phase."

"I call this one *Midnight*," Happy explained.

Megan could see how the title fit. "It's . . . pretty," she said.

"Thanks," Happy muttered, stepping away from the canvas. She pointed to a twin bed on the other side of the room. "That's yours. The mattress is lumpy."

Megan could have guessed which bed was hers. It had white sheets and yellow covers, whereas the other bed . . . all black.

"I'm sure it will be comfortable," Megan said, trying to stay upbeat.

"No," Happy replied. "It won't."

Megan let out a huge sigh. She assured herself everything would be okay. Zach had told her that zombies didn't sleep much, anyway.

"Well," Sam said, "you two can get to know each other later. Megan and I have an appointment with Nurse Karen."

"Nice to meet you," Happy said in a way that made Megan think she didn't mean it.

"Yeah," Megan replied. Happy wasn't anything like Rachel, but Megan didn't have any friends at Zombie Academy. She needed to be nice to Happy. Maybe there was a smile hidden under all that dark face paint. "Want to have lunch together?" Megan asked.

Happy pinched her lips, considering Megan's invitation. "Okay. But the cafeteria food isn't like what you're used to at home."

Megan knew about moldy fruit already, but had a pressing question. "We don't really have to eat brains, do we?"

"On Mondays they serve last year's vegetables," Happy said. "I'll meet you in the dining room at noon."

Spoiled vegetables. That wasn't too bad. And yet, Megan was left to wonder what was on the menu for Tuesday.

POISON APPLE BOOKS

The Dead End

This Totally Bites!

Miss Fortune

Now You See Me...

Midnight Howl

Her Evil Twin

Curiosity Killed the Cat

At First Bite

THRILLING.

BONE-CHILLING.

THESE BOOKS

HAVE BITE!

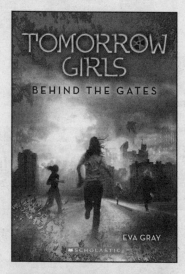

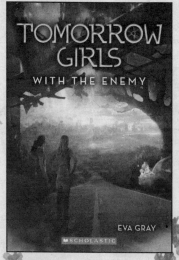